Louisa Heaton lives on Hayling Island, Hampshire, with her husband, four children and a small zoo. She has worked in various roles in the health industry—most recently four years as a Community First Responder, answering 999 calls. When not writing Louisa enjoys other creative pursuits, including reading, quilting and patchwork— usually instead of the things she *ought* to be doing!

Also by Louisa Heaton

Saving the Single Dad Doc
Their Unexpected Babies
The Prince's Cinderella Doc
Pregnant by the Single Dad Doc
Healed by His Secret Baby
The Icelandic Doc's Baby Surprise
Risking Her Heart on the Trauma Doc
A Baby to Rescue Their Hearts

Discover more at millsandboon.co.uk.

TWINS FOR THE NEUROSURGEON

LOUISA HEATON

MILLS & BOON

First published in Great Britain 2021
by Mills & Boon, an imprint of HarperCollins*Publishers* Ltd,
1 London Bridge Street, London, SE1 9GF

www.harpercollins.co.uk

HarperCollins*Publishers*
1st Floor, Watermarque Building,
Ringsend Road, Dublin 4, Ireland

Large Print edition 2022

Twins for the Neurosurgeon © 2021 Louisa Heaton

ISBN: 978-0-263-29368-5

03/22

MIX
Paper from
responsible sources
FSC™ C007454

FALKIRK COUNCIL LIBRARIES

To all the midwives, doctors
and obstetricians who save lives
and ensure healthy deliveries,
as much as they can, every single day.
You are greatly appreciated. x

PROLOGUE

Eleven weeks ago

THE SECOND SHE got through the door to her hotel room, Samantha Gordon kicked off her heels with a heavy sigh and let her bag drop to the floor. In the darkness of her room, she padded over to the big window that revealed the Paris skyline at night in all its wonderful glory.

There was the Eiffel Tower, gleaming in gold, the beating heart of this city. And all around it yellow and red veins of light, as drivers drove their cars to various destinations. The tourists, the city's lifeblood, and the residents were all going about their lives as if nothing incredibly significant had just happened in hers.

How did life just carry on?

Sam envied them their ignorance. Wished that she could be out there with them, taking in the delights of the city one last time. Dining on crêpes, or macarons, or crème brûlée. Walking by the river or the palace, or hoping for one last glimpse of beauty at the Louvre. Sucking up the energy, the culture, the passion and hope within this city and somehow bottling it to take it back home with her to Richmond.

She wished that she could pretend that this day hadn't ever happened at all.

Instead she was here. Standing in the dark. In this hotel room, alone. Knowing that her actions today had resulted in a beautiful girl no longer being in this world. A wonderful young girl. Emmeline. An eleven-year-old who had already been through so much, who had been tired, who had *begged* them not to do another surgery.

But it hadn't been Emmeline's call.

That decision had lain with her parents, and Sam knew that they were somewhere out there in this vibrant city of light, broken, in pieces, also questioning their decision today. Mourning. Grieving. Maybe even blaming each other. Who knew? Would today's decision rip them apart? Emmeline's mother had been sure surgery was the right thing. Her father not so much. It was certainly a decision that would be with them for ever.

Sam knew that. Bad memories had a way of clinging on. Of digging into your psyche, clawing into you with painful ripping talons, changing it, changing *you*. Bad memories were studied, provoked. Feasted on. They popped up when you least expected them to ruin your day. A phantom of the past. Haunting you for ever.

'I'm so sorry, Emmeline,' she whispered, pressing her forehead against the ceiling-to-floor windows. And she told herself, there and then, that she would never forget this girl.

Ever.

She deserved to remember her. She deserved to be reminded of her. The ghost of this girl would remind Sam every day that she needed to be sure about every single decision she made.

A gentle knock at her hotel room door brought her back to the present. She almost didn't answer it. The idea of facing people... seeing anyone...

Sam wanted to ignore it. Wanted to just lie on her bed and stare into space for a while, and maybe later order some food to her room. She'd not eaten very well the last couple of days, having caught a tummy bug. But now she could feel her hunger.

Tomorrow she had to be up early for her flight home at eight-twenty. That meant getting to the airport an hour or so earlier, which meant getting up at… She groaned at the thought of such an early wake-up call. Hiding beneath the quilt seemed like such a wonderful idea right now. Maybe she could phone the airline? Change her flight to a later one? There had to be more than one flight to London tomorrow, right?

'One second!'

She padded across the floor in her bare feet and picked up her bag, hung it off the back of a chair. Then she picked up her heels and placed them off to one side, before peering through the spyhole in the door. She wasn't just going to open her door this late at night when she wasn't expecting anyone.

Yanis?

Yanis Baptiste was one of the neurosurgeons she'd been working with on this exchange between her hospital in Richmond—St Barnabas's, affectionately known as Barney's—and his hospital, Hôpital St Albert.

It was a month-long exchange. Sam and a few other doctors from various hospital departments had come over to Paris, whilst some of the Parisian doctors had gone over to London to work. It was something they'd been doing for a few years, and this year Sam had volunteered to go, having heard so many wonderful stories from other doctors who had taken part. They had informed her of just how much knowledge they had gained from the exchange. Plus, it would be a chance to soak up the local culture. See the sights, too.

Sam was always looking to expand her knowledge. Always trying to find new ways of doing things and learning...

But what was *he* doing here? This late at night?

She opened the door. 'Hey... I wasn't expecting a visit.'

She smiled at him. It was hard not to. Yanis Baptiste was a very handsome man. Dark hair, piercing blue eyes. Cheekbones you could cut yourself on and lips that… Well, the first time she'd met him she could remember thinking that she'd happily suck on his bottom lip. Or bite it.

It had been kind of distracting, working with him, but Sam had behaved herself, despite the constant flirting and the knowledge that they were both single consenting adults.

'There is a tradition here at St Albert that when we lose a patient we raise a glass to celebrate their life.' He held up a bottle of red wine.

Well, if it was *tradition*… Plus, Sam was ready for a drink of something stronger than the tea she'd been about to make herself. And there was no way she was going to raid the mini bar and be faced with an extortionate bill when she left.

She stepped back, opening the door wider. 'Come on in.'

Yanis smiled and stepped past, and she was met by his usual scent—something exotic and masculine. Briefly she closed her eyes to enjoy it, breathing him in, letting it soothe her ragged soul, before opening her eyes again and closing the door.

Yanis was looking for glasses, which he found above the mini bar. 'You like Merlot?'

'Sure.'

She wasn't sure where to sit. There were only two places—the chair next to the small table in the corner, or on the bed—so she just stood, watching him, as he popped the cork effortlessly and poured them both a glass.

He handed one to her and raised his own. 'To Emmeline.'

Hearing him say the young girl's name caused a lump in her throat. Reminded her of that sweet girl's smile.

'To Emmeline.' She clinked her glass against his and took a sip. The wine was beautiful and ran over her tongue with a gentle caress of flavour.

She looked at him over the rim of her glass, drinking in the sculpted beauty of his face. He had such expressive eyes. The kind she could lose herself in if she wasn't careful.

'You were upset when you left.'

He stared at her so intently... It wasn't an

accusation. More of an observation, inviting her to speak about how she felt.

'Yes, well…losing a patient will do that to you.'

'It is always a difficult thing.'

She needed to sit down, so she sank onto the edge of the foot of her bed. 'It just hit me hard, you know? She didn't want that surgery. She'd had so many already. She was tired. Done. She didn't want it any more—the fight. How many times did you tell me you'd gone in before?'

Yanis sat down next to her. 'Three.' His voice was sad.

'Three times… Three times in her short life that poor girl had gone through brain surgery to scrape out a recurring tumour. No wonder she'd had enough!'

It hadn't been just the trauma of surgery she'd needed to get past each time, but the recovery from surgery, too. Each one taking longer than the last.

'We could not leave it. You know that. Doing so would have resulted in her losing function and dying. It would have been a terrible way to go.'

the comfort that only another person could provide. Yearning for the warmth and the security and the safety. Yearning for a connection that she had not had for a long time.

Being here in Paris had made her feel so alone—something she'd not expected when she'd first packed her bags for a month in the city of love. She'd imagined meeting some French waiter or barman. Someone who would catch her eye and maybe provide some fun and laughter in amongst the hard work she would do here. A lighter side to her life. A brightness. A connection. Fun.

But she'd been so busy at the hospital, so exhausted when she came back to the hotel each night, she'd not really had time to sightsee or enjoy the city for what it was. But Yanis she knew. They'd known each other only for a month, but they had worked together a lot in that time, and she trusted him as a professional.

So she sank against Yanis's chest, sighing heavily into the warmth of him, the strength of his arms around her, and closed her eyes in bliss as he stroked away her concerns and her cares, one hand on her back, the other stroking her hair. Her tears dried up and she realised they were swaying gently. He was rocking her, soothing her, and it felt so good and so right that she almost didn't want it to end.

Lifting her head to look at him, to smile and say thank you, she was suddenly caught in the tractor beam of his intense gaze and the words got stuck in her throat.

Yanis looked down at her with a question in his eyes, a want and need of his own, and suddenly she realised just how upset that he must be, too. Yanis had *known* Emmeline. Much better than Sam had. He had worked on her for every surgery, had watched her grow over the last few years, had no doubt hoped for a better outcome than the one they'd experienced today. And yet here he was, comforting *her*.

She could see, sense, *feel* just how much Yanis needed this, too.

'Yanis...'

'Oui?'

'Will you kiss me?'

She'd never in her whole life asked a man to kiss her before, but she had to right now.

She knew Yanis wouldn't do so without her giving her consent first. He would never assume that she wanted him to kiss her just because they were comforting each other. But something had changed within her as he'd embraced her. It was as if her whole body had come alive.

She'd felt so weary and tired when she'd made it back to her hotel room—hours operating on someone's brain would do that to a person—but now all that world-weariness had gone and she felt alive for the first time in ages. She just knew that she wanted something to happen between them. It felt right. This was her last night in Paris. That was all she knew and that was all she needed to know. If they were going to celebrate a life, then why not enjoy the one they were living right now? Take a chance…strike whilst the iron was hot.

Who could truly know how much time they had left on this earth?

Yanis was here with her in this hotel room and she deserved to enjoy him as much as he would enjoy her. Why not comfort each other?

He placed a finger beneath her chin, lifting it ever so slightly as he stared deeply into her eyes. She saw his pupils, large and dark with arousal, and in that moment she knew she had never looked into a man's eyes that were so intense. So beautiful. So exotic.

The feel of his lips lightly brushing over her own sent fireworks exploding throughout her body, and a heat began to build within her as her hands began to clutch at his clothes.

Don't let me go.

His lips trailed down one side of her neck, feather-light, gentle, and the occasional quick touch of his hot tongue against her skin made her nerve endings dance in delight.

Her heart began to pound within her chest. She needed this. This oblivion. Being with Yanis like this would take away all the pain of losing Emmeline and would, for a brief while at least, take away her own past, her own regrets, her own grief.

His lips found hers again and he deepened the kiss. She began to loosen the knot of his dark tie, her fingers hungry for the buttons of his shirt, so she could get past those, feel the wonder of his skin. Feel the heat of him.

The strength. The flexing of muscles moving beneath flesh.

She shrugged out of her blouse, felt Yanis's hand at the zip of her skirt before it fell to the floor. He lowered her gently onto the bed and she pulled him close, not willing to be apart from him for a second, arching towards him, meeting him, relishing the weight of him above her, his skin against hers.

His body was a delight, and exactly as she'd imagined. From the very first day at St Albert she had noticed Yanis—before they'd even been introduced.

He was tall, at least six feet, and his straight, dark hair was exquisitely styled to look as if he'd just been dragged out of bed. But he was still groomed enough to look professional. Just watching him move, she knew that he looked after himself. Broad shoulders, a trim, neat waist in his slim-fit shirts, trousers that accentuated his backside and thighs.

He was a man who knew how to dress for his shape. Or was that just a French thing? That innate sense of style that all French people seemed to have so effortlessly? It would not have surprised her to see him strolling down a catwalk, or even to find out he modelled in his spare time. She'd seen the way people looked at him. Nurses, patients, other doctors, even one or two men had cast an appreciative eye over the delectable Yanis Baptiste. A double take, a second look just to make sure that their eyes hadn't been deceived.

And he was *single*. How that was possible she didn't know, but right now she was very glad that he was—especially as his mouth was doing such wonderful things as it trailed over her stomach.

Did he notice her scars? Did he wonder? Did he have questions? She felt shame begin its deep burn and suddenly wanted to hide, to cover herself, but that feeling went away when he simply carried on, without stopping or pausing. Without speaking.

He said nothing as his lips trailed lower, his tongue lapping at her belly button, his teeth nibbling ever so gently over her hip bone, his fingers hooking into her underwear and sliding them down, so she ignored her feelings and pushed them away.

She lifted her hips to make it easier for him

and closed her eyes in ecstasy as his mouth trailed up her left inner thigh.

Her fingers caught in his hair...

And then... *Oh, yes!*

She simply lost herself. It was as if all thoughts vanished, all cares were washed away, and all upset and shame disappeared, to be replaced by wonder and heat and delicious excitement as she thrust her body against his mouth, never wanting it to stop, never wanting these sensations to end. He drove her onwards, upwards, higher and higher as his tongue slicked over her flesh, and just as she thought she might explode, his lips came back to her own and she tasted herself upon him.

'Sam...we should protect ourselves.'

She nodded. 'I'm on the pill. Do you have a condom?'

He shook his head. 'I didn't come here expecting to...' He looked down at her body, smiled. 'I haven't been with a woman for a long time.'

'I've not been with a man for a long time.'

She grinned and pulled him towards her. Urging him on, wrapping her legs around his waist, she gasped with pleasure as he slowly filled her with the long length of him and began to move slowly, watching her every expression.

Sam gazed into his eyes, holding on tight, riding the wave that was coming. She was unable to look away, not wanting to look away, needing to have that connection, to see into his soul, for him to see into hers.

Briefly, she worried about what he might see…worried that he might sense she was broken and could never be fixed and because of that he might stop. So she closed her eyes to him, denying him that kind of access, and buried her face in his neck as her body began its ascent.

She felt the build of it, the surge, the sparks of electricity, the fizzing of nerve endings as the current suddenly exploded and she cried out, clutching him tight, her nails scraping his back as he came, too. She felt him thrust even deeper, stronger, and then, after a few breaths, he slowly stilled and began to kiss and caress her collarbone.

The delicate kisses were a balm for the frenzy of before.

He pulled back to look into her eyes. 'Are you all right, *ma chérie*?'

She nodded, smiling, but unable to open her eyes and look at him. She suddenly felt ashamed. Ashamed and fearful over what they had done.

Had he seen the real her? The Sam Gordon she liked to keep hidden? Had he glimpsed her secret?

Now that it was over—now that she'd had what she needed in that moment so she could forget—she wanted him gone.

Before he could ask too many questions.

CHAPTER ONE

Present day

THERE WAS NOTHING quite like the feeling of stepping into an operating theatre. This was the place where the magic happened. Where the fight for life was not just black or white, but many shades of grey. Here, the inevitable could be fought. Here, the surgeon's skill battled disease, or old age, or trauma, and triumphed.

The operating theatres were probably the most important rooms in the hospital. Not that Sam thought any less of the wards, where patients recovered, or the rehabilitation department, where patients relearned old skills so that they could return to something resembling normal life. It was just that in Theatre was where the battle began, and without her skills, her knowledge and her ability, those patients could not begin down their road to recovery.

Walking into Theatre scrubbed and sterile, ready for her gown and her gloves, her mask and headset, was a ritual, a practice that made her feel as if she had all the power in the world. And *control.*

It was a heady feeling, and one that she had been determined to have her entire life.

Her patient already lay on the table, anaesthetised and connected to a respirator. Beside the anaesthetist, machines beeped and gasped, monitoring oxygen rates, heart rate, blood pressure and temperature.

'Let's run it,' she said, as a nurse fastened her gown at her side.

'Dante Jackson, four months of age, here for a shunt due to hydrocephalus.'

'You've checked the tags?'

'Yep. It's the right patient on the table.'

She nodded, glad that all seemed correct. Over on the wall were Dante's recent scans, lit up from behind, and she examined them one last time. She didn't really need to. She knew exactly what was happening inside this little boy's head. But it was a ritual. She always did it. She checked and double-checked. She made sure. There was no room for mistakes or surprises in her theatre. This was a room in which she was always in control.

'Scalpel.' She held out her hand and her nurse assist placed the blade into her hand.

Time to begin.

As ever, she muttered her little mantra beneath her face mask. 'Above all, do no harm…' Then louder, for the rest of the staff, she said, 'Let's make a difference, everyone.'

She felt the rest of the theatre team relax, even saw a few eyes crinkling at the corners as they smiled. It was a habit, a practice that enveloped them all together as a team. Almost a good luck routine. It was like a footballer always wearing the same pair of socks for a match, or an actor always cracking his neck before going on stage. It made Sam feel better and everyone else, too, because it made them feel she was on her game.

Which she was—even if she did feel a bit off today…

It was the strangest thing, but she felt sure it was nothing, really.

Whenever Sam felt ill, or off in some way,

she always told herself that it was nothing. That she was imagining it, or that it was just a psychosomatic echo left over from childhood. Of course, in reality she knew that she *could* get sick. People did all the time. Colds. The flu. Headaches. Fever. But she was a type-A personality and she always pushed through it. She'd take paracetamol to stop the pain or bring down her fever. She'd push through a cold and take decongestants. She never let illness stop her doing what she was meant to be doing.

But today she felt a little...

It was difficult to pin down exactly how she felt. She'd felt tired a lot just lately. She'd had a few headaches, but had put it down to her workload over recent weeks. They'd been a surgeon down, and waiting for the hospital to employ a replacement, so in the meantime she'd been working extra-hard, extra-long hours, long days, completing the work of two neurosurgeons, with two neuro lists, and it had been a real struggle.

But she'd felt on top of it, and she'd even received a pat on the back from the chief of neurosurgery for the way she'd been handling the workload.

Sam looked down on the patient's shaved head—he'd barely even begun to grow thick hair—and made the first incision. Sure. Precise. There was nothing wrong with her hands! She was as steady as a rock.

'How are we looking, Aarav?' she asked the anaesthetist.

'All good.'

'Excellent.'

She was hoping to place a ventriculoperitoneal shunt into little Dante, which would work by taking the extra fluid out of his brain and shunting it down to his belly, where it would be absorbed.

'Drill, please.'

She held out her hand for the instrument and as she did so suddenly felt nauseous. That wasn't something she usually experienced—and most definitely not in Theatre. In Theatre, the rest of the world ceased to exist until the battle was over. This new sensation, in a world that was usually under her total control, threw her.

'Could someone get me some water?' she asked, feeling all eyes suddenly on her.

Sam never asked for water. She never asked for music. She liked the silence. The reassuring rhythm of the machines was all the tune she needed to hear. This odd diversion was something that would be noted, and with all the attention she felt herself grow a little hot.

Nerves, that's all it is. You've had a lot on. This is normal. Natural. Ignore it. Besides, you want to be on top form today.

The new surgeon would be arriving this morning. Was probably already here. Filling in paperwork, most likely, getting an ID card sorted, being given the welcome pack from the chief of neurosurgery, Elliot Parker. Elliot liked to give his new recruits a welcome meeting—liked to talk them through what he expected, what his vision for the department was and all that jazz.

Sam had passed Elliot in the corridor earlier and told him that when he'd finished terrorising the new surgeon he should send him to her theatre to join in. She might even let him assist. Get his hands dirty straight away and make him feel part of the team by showing trust in regard to her patient. Besides, this shunt surgery was simple enough. It was something Sam could do in her sleep. And it would be a good excuse to assess her new colleague. Make sure he was right for Barney's.

A team couldn't run smoothly if there was someone on it who couldn't pull their weight. They each needed to know that they could trust and rely on each other. Especially in a place like this, where it was life and death every day. This new neuro was a good guy, too. She'd heard of his work. David Emery had recently published a paper on burr hole techniques that had been absolutely fascinating, and she was looking forward to working with him.

She took a steadying breath as she placed the equipment and drilled a small hole through the skull, determined to ignore the churning in her stomach. She carried on working. Steady. Sure. Each movement a practised piece of perfect choreography. It helped her to focus…the familiarity, the sequence of steps needed to place the shunt.

A nurse arrived with a glass of water,

equipped with a straw, and lowered her mask slightly so Sam could take a long drink. That felt better. Her mouth was no longer dry and that weird taste in her mouth had gone, if only for a moment.

Refreshed, she continued to work, aware of the theatre door behind her opening, of someone approaching the table opposite her. She looked up to welcome David Emery.

'Good morning! Glad you could join me...' She stopped as her eyes met those of someone she hadn't expected. Someone she remembered all too well. They were unmistakable. Icy blue, framed by long, dark lashes.

Was it really him?

It couldn't be!

Could it?

What had happened to David Emery? Was he still coming?

'Yanis?'

'Bonjour. How are you?'

She saw his eyes crinkle, saw them gleam in amusement at how shocked she was. For a moment she struggled to gather her thoughts, trying to push aside the memories she had of Yanis. Of them together in her hotel room.

Making love in the dark. Her mind felt as if it had been cast into a raging storm. She needed to ground herself.

'This is Dante. Four months old and in for a ventriculoperitoneal shunt. Have you ever done one of these before?'

Sam was aware that her voice sounded shaky. She couldn't meet his gaze. Couldn't look at anyone. It was as if her body *remembered*. Their last encounter, such a passionate one, had ended in such a state of confusion when, after their lovemaking session, she had practically kicked him out of her hotel room, afraid that she had exposed too much of herself to him. Given away too many secrets.

'I have.'

She needed to get control of this situation! This was *her* theatre. Her patient. Dante was the most important person in the room, not him. And this was not the place for second guesses and doubts. But she could feel her reaction to Yanis. The trembling in her body.

'Then let's see what you can do.' She passed him the tools, feeling that it would put her in a stronger position and would not alert anyone to how he had affected her by just walking into the room. Would not let anyone see how her hands had begun to shake.

Damn him!

'Water, please.' The nurse presented her with the straw again and briefly lifted her mask for her, so that she might drink. 'Thank you.'

When she turned around again to face Yanis, he was already at work. His face was a mask of concentration as he perfectly placed the shunt and attached the valve. He checked to see that there was correct drainage of the cerebrospinal fluid and then began his preparations to close. The scrub nurse assisted him as Sam watched, maintaining a careful eye on everything.

'I wasn't expecting to see you today,' she said.

'*Non?* It was a last-minute change. Elliot's first choice turned down the post at the last minute. I did not.'

Yanis, as she already knew, was an exceptional neurosurgeon and would be a brilliant fit for the team here at Barney's. She'd watched this man in action many times. He worked the same way she did. Had the same instincts. He strove for perfection in every surgery he undertook. She had no doubt that Dante was in excellent hands.

'Aarav? Everything all right at your end?' she asked, trying to establish a modicum of control in the room.

'BP is running steady. He's dealing with the surgery very well.'

'Good.'

As Yanis closed, she felt a wave of heat wash over her and she swayed slightly on her feet. What the heck was *that*? It startled her, worried at her, and she turned to the nurse so she could dab at her brow with a cloth.

Sam never sweated like this in a surgery. Even when something went wrong and she had to leap into emergency protocols to fend off a bleed, or administer CPR. She remained steady and sure, reliant on her knowledge and her training being at their peak. She felt adrenaline rushes, sure, but this heady mix she was feeling right now was all because of *him*.

When the last stitch was in and Yanis turned to thank everyone, Sam knew she had to get out of the room before his gaze turned on her. She couldn't stand there a moment longer.

I need some fresh air.

Yanking off her gloves, mask and then her gown, she pressed the treadle foot for the bin and threw them all in, then headed to the scrub room to clean up. Maybe she could get in and out of there before Yanis followed and caught up with her. If she could just get some time to think this over…think this through.

How was she going to deal with having him here? She had opened herself up to this man. Had allowed him to see her body. Her soul. She had exposed herself to him and he knew things. She knew he did. Even if he didn't know what they meant, he had seen her scars and she had allowed that to happen thinking that she would never see him again. Thinking that, believing that, it was a safe thing to do. She had allowed herself to find comfort in his arms, but it had only been meant to be a one-time thing!

Now he was her colleague. Permanently.

Sam scrubbed at her hands and nails, eager to get done, keen to get away from the way she was feeling, from the warmth of her body, the light-headedness that was affecting her, the churn of her stomach. Her legs felt weak, her whole body felt drained, and what with the shock of his arrival, it was all—

'Samantha.'

That voice! Velvety… Soft liquid richness with a French accent tempering and sweetening all his words. It was as if his voice was an actual caress. A balm to her tortured soul. Yet it was also the cause of its discomfort right now. It was a confusing juxtaposition.

She closed her eyes and paused in her scrubbing for just a moment. She had to get control! She turned to look at him, knowing she needed to create distance between them after their last intimate, close-up encounter.

'Mr Baptiste.'

He'd taken off his headcover and mask, and now she was reminded of the true impact of the man. He was exactly as she remembered. It hadn't been a dream, or an exaggeration. He truly was as stunning as she recalled.

But just because we've slept together once, it doesn't mean anything. It wasn't a connection. It wasn't lust. We just comforted each other—that's all and he's probably with someone now.

Surprisingly, that last thought did not bring her comfort. Only awkwardness.

'I didn't know you were planning on coming to Richmond.'

'I wasn't. But the opportunity presented itself, along with a raise in salary and a chance to perform some research, and my brother said I could live in his flat until I found my own place.'

'Your brother lives in *Richmond*?' How had she not even known he had a brother? What on earth had they talked about back in Paris?

Oh, that's right, we talked about patients and surgeries because I was panicked by how stunning he was and it seemed an easy way to keep my mind on task.

'*Oui.* Well, he did. Now Luca is off trapping and radio-tagging rhino in South Africa.'

She turned off the water and grabbed at some paper towels to dry herself. 'Rhino?'

'He is a veterinary surgeon.'

'Is everyone a surgeon of some kind in your family?'

Yanis smiled, and it did strange things to her tummy. Why was her heart racing? Why did she feel so shaky? Why couldn't her stomach settle? And what was that strange roaring, rushing noise in her ears?

She saw Yanis answer her, but it was almost as if noise had been muted. The rushing sound in her ears became louder and she found it hard to focus. She looked up at Yanis, tried to focus on his features, tried to use him as some sort of anchor. But everything was beginning to blur, and the world had begun to darken at the edges, and she realised much too late that she was going to pass out.

The last thing she saw was Yanis frown and reach for her, before everything went black and her world became blissfully peaceful once again.

He caught her before she hit the floor and in one rapid movement scooped his arm under her legs and carried her out of the scrub room. He had no idea why she had fainted like that, but he wondered if maybe she hadn't eaten that morning and had low blood sugar.

He determined to check. Surgeons often thought they were machines and could carry on for hours, putting their patients first, but if they didn't look after themselves then what use were they to the people in their care?

A scrub nurse carrying a surgical pack stopped and stared. 'What's happened to Sam?'

'Fainted. Tell me where I can lie her down.'

She was getting heavy in his arms, but that didn't matter. He would carry her as long as she needed. He knew how driven Sam was. He'd seen it. Watched her. He had sometimes been amazed by her, and clearly she'd been trying to pursue her goal of becoming chief of neurosurgery one day by working herself into the ground.

She needed to rest. To eat. To drink. And then he would run a blood test to see what she might be deficient in.

'In here.'

The nurse opened a door, allowing him into the room where pre-operative patients sometimes waited, before being taken into Theatre. Right now it was empty, and he gently laid her down on a bed, then grabbed the bed control and raised the lower end, so that her legs were higher than her heart. He placed an oxygen mask over her face and turned on the air flow at the wall.

He stared at her face. At the fine arches of her natural eyebrows and her high, rounded cheekbones. The spread of her flaming hair against the whiteness of the pillow reminded him of that night together.

'Can you get me something to test her blood sugar with? And the kit for a basic blood test?'

The nurse nodded and hurried from the room.

Alone with Sam, he leaned over her, close to her face, and made his voice soft and soothing. 'Samantha? Wake up.'

She was so pale. Paler than normal. Normally her alabaster skin looked perfect against those long locks of auburn flame, but right now her skin had an ill tinge to it that he did not like. *Had* she been working too hard? Trying to fulfil the hours of the surgeon they'd not had until his arrival? Had she taken on too much? Doctors did it all the time. He'd seen them burn out. He sincerely hoped that this wasn't the case here.

He'd been thrilled to accept the post at St Barnabas's. Although, unwilling to leave his own department in the lurch to travel to Richmond for interview, he had asked Elliot to interview him by video call. Since Covid, the world had adapted, and people had discovered that so much that used to be done in person could just as easily be done online. He was grateful for it. He'd worried about finding a place in London, but then Luca had come to the rescue there, and everything had fallen into place.

Discovering that Sam was still here had been thrilling to hear, after their friendship and intimate connection in Paris, though he was still a little perturbed as to why she had thrown him out afterwards the way she had. As if she'd been embarrassed. He couldn't understand why. She was perfect. Beautiful.

He'd thought about her often since that night, but told himself that she was off-limits to him, what with the way she'd thrown him out. Such a clear message that she had regrets. Maybe she didn't date co-workers? He'd decided he would respect her boundaries and offer friendship only.

But now? He had almost been amused at how shocked she'd been to see him in her theatre. And glad that he'd affected her so. That he'd made an impression. He'd even enjoyed it.

But fainting? That he was not so pleased about. It told him that she hadn't been looking after herself lately, and he suspected she'd already had some past health concerns.

He'd not been blind that night. He'd seen all those scars. Surgical scars. Laparoscopic marks on her abdomen. An appendectomy scar. She'd been through something. A long time ago, judging by the silvery nature of the marks—they were almost invisible. But surgeons noticed those things the way phlebotomists noticed good veins. They were trained to. And although he'd said nothing that night, perhaps now that he was here and working with her he could keep an eye on her to make sure she took care of herself?

Sam groaned softly.

He reached for her hand and squeezed her fingers. 'Hey...that's it. Open your eyes.'

He saw her frown, then blink, before opening her eyes wide and pulling the oxygen mask off her face. 'What happened?'

'You fainted.'

'Fainted? No.'

She tried to sit up, but he gently pushed her back down against the pillows.

'Stay there for a moment. You have not been looking after yourself, Samantha.'

She glared at him.

It was his turn to frown. Why was she being so hostile? Was she embarrassed about having passed out? He'd only been trying to make a light-hearted joke.

At that moment the scrub nurse returned with the equipment he'd asked for. He smiled a thank-you. *'Merci.'*

'What's that for?' Sam asked.

'To check you over.'

'I'm fine.' She tried to sit up again, and swung her legs out of the bed, but when she sat up she paused and went a little green-looking. 'Ugh...'

'Lie back, *mon amie*. Let me take care of you.'

'I feel sick.'

'That is normal after fainting.' He turned to the scrub nurse. 'Could you wet some paper towel for her head?'

The nurse nodded and brought over some wet blue paper towel and draped it on Sam's forehead.

'Thank you.' She laid her head back against the pillow. 'What tests are you taking?'

'Blood sugar. Vitamins and minerals. A basic blood test.' He glanced at her, thinking for a moment about a possibility he would ask any young woman about if she had fainted in front of him. 'And HCG. Do you consent?'

She raised a sardonic eyebrow. 'Are you going to let me off this bed if I say no?'

He smiled at her. *'Non.'*

'You can't force me to do anything against my will.'

He continued to smile, knowing he would win this small battle. 'That is true.'

'So I could just sit up and wait for you to go. Or wait until I get beeped to take care of a patient.'

'Yes. But then I would have to go to Elliot with my concerns.'

'You wouldn't...'

He met her gaze, deadly serious now. 'Try me. I take patient care very seriously indeed, and I'm sure Elliot would not be happy if his best neurosurgeon fainted in Theatre over an open brain.'

Sam glared at him, then closed her eyes again, pressing the wet towel against her head. 'Fine. I consent. But I never expected you to be the sort to tell tales.'

She held out her arm.

Smiling at his small victory against this very stubborn woman whom he admired so much, he prepped her fingertip first, to take the blood sugar sample. As he'd suspected, her blood sugar was very low.

'You need to eat.'

'Right now, I think it would come straight back up.'

'You still feel sick?'

'It's just tiredness. I've felt that way for a while. It's what happens when you work too hard.'

'Perhaps.'

'Well, what else could it be?' she asked irritably.

As he slid the needle into her arm, and began applying tubes to the Vacutainer system, he considered his next words very carefully. 'Well, you've either not been taking care of yourself very well, or you have an illness, or…'

She looked at him. 'Or what?'

'Or you're pregnant.'

She seemed to stare at him for an age, before laughing nervously. 'Pregnant? That's ridiculous. I…'

She stopped talking and looked away. He saw her do some rapid period maths.

'No. It can't be…'

'When was your last period, Sam?'

He felt a frisson of something ripple through his own body at the way she'd just reacted. This might not be his problem. Just because they'd slept together nearly three months ago, it did not mean she could be pregnant with *his* child. She could have slept with someone else after him. Eight weeks ago, maybe. Six weeks ago. Who knew? Besides, it might not even be pregnancy!

But the look on her face unnerved him a little.

'They've always been irregular. I'm on the pill. I told you...'

The pill was good. Could he relax, then? 'You take it regularly?' he asked.

'Yes. I try to.'

He removed the needle from her arm and pressed a small cotton wool ball into her antecubital fossa. 'Press here.'

He turned to label the tubes and then slipped them into a bag to send them off to Pathology, his mind whirring like a cyclone.

'Did you take it regularly when you were in Paris?' he asked quietly.

She met his gaze. 'You think I'm pregnant with your baby?'

He shrugged. 'I have no idea. Have you slept with anyone else since?'

'That's none of your damned business!'

'Okay. Let's see what the results say.'

He was not offended by her defensiveness. He understood it. If pregnancy *was* the cause of her fainting and feeling ill, Sam would be greatly affected. Her life changed in an instant. It was no wonder she was getting upset with him. Though if she'd been taking the pill properly they should be fine.

She nodded. 'It'll be negative. I'm sure of it.'

But she didn't *look* sure of it, and inwardly he was worried. Worried that the test would come back and show that Sam's HCG levels were raised. Worried that she could be carrying his child in her womb.

Because if that was the case then his new start, the new life that he'd hoped to begin when he arrived in Richmond, would soon be destroyed.

CHAPTER TWO

LITTLE DANTE WAS doing well after his surgery. Sam had checked on him and her other post-operative patients before a quick trip to the hospital cafeteria to get something to eat. She'd stood over the counter, looking at the various hot and cold offerings, not sure what she wanted to eat that she would keep down, and opted for a large chocolate chip cookie to help her blood sugar and a small bottle of fresh orange juice. Because, well… Healthy stuff would balance out the sugar-laden cookie. Plus, they were both quick to consume.

She hadn't even sat. She'd simply bought them and now stood in the corridor, quickly eating and drinking.

She didn't want to stay in any one place, even for a little while. It was better, she felt, to keep moving, because she was trying to avoid Yanis and those questioning eyes of his.

Yanis Baptiste. Here. *Permanently!* In *her* hospital.

Bewilderment was a fine word to explain how she was feeling. Never in a million years had she ever expected that he would come back into her life, and it was a complication that she didn't need right now.

She'd fainted. *Fainted!* Sam had never fainted in her entire life, and she'd been through some pretty harrowing stuff. To faint in front of Yanis, of all people... And now he had this ridiculous idea that she could be pregnant. It was impossible, wasn't it? She was on the pill and she'd slept with Yanis three months ago. There'd have been signs... there'd have been—

Sam let out a breath as her mind helpfully provided the evidence that she had dismissed as just being overworked. Tiredness. Today's nausea. Headaches. The bloating which she'd put down to eating a few weird food combinations...

But all that had to be coincidence, right? Doctors worked odd hours... They grabbed what they could, when they could. It didn't always make sense, but sometimes you just wanted the calories, no matter where they came from. And a bowl of cereal was fabulous at any time of day or night.

She rubbed at her abdomen through her scrubs. Was it rounder? Had she put on weight? Maybe a little. It was hard to tell when you lived in scrubs for most of the day. Those things were elasticated or had a pull-string around the waist. Nothing was fitted.

And I had that tummy bug in Paris.

She couldn't be a mother. Absolutely not— no way. It wasn't in her life plan. It wasn't on her to-do list. There wasn't a maternal bone in her body. Sam's own mother had seen to that.

But she didn't want to stand here ruminating on *her.* There were things to do, and she couldn't stand idle whilst she waited for her blood test results to come back. A part of her didn't want to know the results. Living in blissful ignorance sounded great right now.

Thankfully, at that very moment her pager went off. She was needed in A & E to assess a trauma patient.

She threw the cookie wrapper and the juice bottle in the nearest bin as if she was playing basketball, applauded herself for getting them both in first time, and headed for the stairwell.

The patient was a middle-aged man who'd had a fall from a height of six feet onto concrete, just over a week ago. Max Winshaw had presented to A & E then, via ambulance, and initial scans of his head and neck had been clear. But now he had been brought in again by his wife, Cara, who was concerned that there was something more going on.

'He's not right, Doctor.'

'In what way?'

Sam was observing her patient carefully. He lay back on the cubicle bed, one arm over his eyes as if he had a headache.

'He's been really irritable from this pain in his head, which he says is getting worse, and paracetamol doesn't touch it. He's got no energy, and he says his vision is weird.'

'Explain "weird".' She pulled out her pen torch and examined the pupilar reaction in Max's eyes.

'Blurry…out of focus sometimes. But it's the pain in his head that's most worrying, and this morning he's been sick.'

Sam nodded. 'His last scans were clear, but considering the mechanism of his injury and the symptoms, I suggest we do another immediate scan to be on the safe side—just to make sure he hasn't developed a slow bleed.'

'Into his brain?' Cara covered her mouth. 'Oh… You think it might be serious?'

'Let's see what the CT scans say. I'm going to order one right now, okay? A nurse will come and take you through. Max? I want you to stay on this bed.'

He nodded and groaned. He didn't look good.

Sam ordered the scan and then had a thought. If Max needed surgery, she would take him into Theatre. That would be a good way to pass the time until her blood results came back in. But then again, she had just recently fainted. Perhaps doing surgery herself right now wasn't the best idea? If she called Yanis, she could give the case to him—no matter how much that would grate on her nerves—and the patient would be in secure hands. *And* she would know exactly where Yanis was, and wouldn't have to worry about running into him unnecessarily.

She turned to a nurse. 'Could you page Mr Baptiste from Neurosurgery for the Winshaw case, please?'

'Of course.'

'Thanks.'

Sam hated giving over any surgery she considered her own, but right now it seemed the sensible thing to do. Even though she felt better since eating, and she didn't think she would faint again. She'd simply been hungry, and then there'd been the shock of seeing Yanis. Somehow she'd passed out, but she was fine now and felt perfectly well, if a little tired. But patient care came first for Sam, no matter how much she wanted to claim this patient as hers.

When Yanis finally strode into the emergency department, Sam watched with mild amusement as the female staff and a couple of the patients watched him pass with a look of admiration. Sam smiled. He certainly could have that effect if you weren't used to

such fine features, and those eyes and cheekbones were a sight to behold indeed.

'Hi. Thanks for consulting on this case
with me,' she said.

'No problem at all.'

'I hope I didn't tear you away from anything important?'

'I'm good. How can I help?'

Sam filled him in on the case as much as
she could, showing him the previous scans
on the computer. As they talked, the second
set of scans appeared, and they instantly saw
the problem.

'Subdural haematoma.'

'With marked midline shift.' Yanis pointed.
'He needs immediate surgery.'

'I think you should take the lead on this
one,' said Sam.

He nodded. 'My pleasure. Do you want to
assist?'

No. That was what she intended to say. The
whole point of this was to put Yanis in Theatre, so she knew where he was and could
move unencumbered around the hospital
until her blood results came back and exon-

erated her. Then she could go back to being normal.

But the one thing she hadn't bet on was her own personality and drive, and her need to be involved and in control. She loved Theatre. It was difficult to give up an opportunity to be in one.

'Sure,' she said, but inwardly she was berating herself, figuring she'd now have to spend an hour or two with Yanis in a very small space indeed.

With nowhere to run and nowhere to hide.

Yanis stepped forward. 'Are we all ready?' he asked the theatre team.

There were nods of assent.

'Do we have any classical music?'

A nurse nodded and turned on the player.

Something soothing and lyrical began to issue softly from the speakers and Sam smiled beneath her mask.

She'd forgotten he liked classical music. When they'd first met in Paris, and she'd shared her first theatre with him, she'd expected someone like him to prefer heavy rock blasting from the speakers, but she'd been wrong. And watching Yanis operate, his hands and his fingers expertly and delicately operating on a brain whilst heavenly music played, was a sight to behold. His focus was a thing of beauty, and those intense eyes of his, when they were all you could see above the mask, were...hypnotic. It was like watching a craftsman.

She admired his skill and abilities, and knew she found them attractive. So why on earth had she agreed to come into Theatre with him?

He began the craniotomy. The part of surgery that temporarily removed a bone flap from the skull, to allow access to the brain. He worked steadily. Surely. With no hesitation.

Sam liked watching him work. Liked watching his hands. The way he manipulated the tools. She found herself stealing glimpses at his face, wondering what he was thinking.

There was no sign of apprehension on his face. No hint of worry of any kind that he might have got her pregnant. That he might be facing fatherhood.

But perhaps normal people didn't fear becoming a parent?

Sam knew she was different. The idea that she might become a mother was almost impossible to get her head around. She had a career. A vocation. She planned on becoming chief in a few years! Nowhere in her ten-year plan was there a gap created for maternity leave! It simply wasn't going to happen.

The blip she'd experienced today was simply that. A blip. She'd worked too hard, hadn't eaten right, hadn't looked after herself properly having worked so hard to show Elliot what she was capable of. He'd marvelled at her ability to get through her surgical lists, even clapped her on the back a few times, and each time she'd received praise from him she had felt so proud. So noticed. So marvellous. It had made her feel *good*.

Approval was something she craved. There was no way in hell she was going to walk away from something she had fought so long for. She couldn't be pregnant! Her body was playing tricks on her. Acting up. And God only knew she was used to that. It was all a lie. Worries manifesting themselves as symptoms that Yanis had simply imagined could be something else.

Of course the blood test would come back negative.

Max's bleed could now be seen through his dura. Sam hoped it would be a simple case of Yanis opening the dura and removing the clot with suction. However, she knew that though the operation might be simple enough, Max's recovery would be anything but. There was a high mortality rate with this kind of damage. They could fight all they wanted to get rid of this clot and get him through surgery, but anything could take him down afterwards. Brain oedema. New bleeds. Infection. Seizures. An increase in intercranial pressure. They'd have to monitor him closely in the ICU afterwards...

'Suction.'

Yanis slowly and carefully began to remove the clot, and they were all able to quickly see where the bleed had originated. Sam worked quickly to take control of the bleeding and repair the site. She and Yanis had done this before in Paris, and they worked well together. Staying out of each other's way but knowing exactly what the other was doing, knowing what they needed to do, what angle they required to work from, and then adapting their own position.

There was something beautiful about this surgery. About the way they worked. It was as if the rest of the world had slipped away and all there was left was the patient, Yanis and Sam, operating in some kind of bubble. She forgot the music, forgot the other staff, didn't hear the beep of the machines or the clank and clink of instruments as they were placed back on trays. It was like a dance. A tango. Two people working independently to create something beautiful.

'Bleeding has stopped. Good work, Samantha.'

She smiled at his praise and met his eyes. She wanted to say something. Anything. But it was as if her throat had stopped working. All she could feel was the pounding of her heart in her chest and the dryness in her mouth. His gaze made her feel all aflutter, and she had to look away in an attempt to try to regain control.

What was happening to her? Why did he

have the ability to affect her like this? It hadn't happened in Paris.

But you hadn't slept with him then. Not until that final night.

And she'd only done so then because she'd known she would never have to face him again.

She'd thought she could let her barriers down, accept his comfort, enjoy what he offered.

She'd wanted him. She couldn't lie about that.

And now temptation was back in her life, and maybe her body was telling her it would like to get to know him again, because it knew how good it could be with him?

Yes, well... My body used to say a lot of things, and look where that got me.

Yanis replaced the bone flap and closed up, and they both stepped away from the table to go and scrub down.

'I think that went very smoothly,' he said.

She nodded. 'We'll need to keep a close eye on him in Recovery.'

'I always keep a close eye on my patients. Speaking of which—how are you feeling?'

She laughed. 'I'm not your patient, Yanis.'

'Whilst we're waiting for those blood results, technically you are. Until I discharge you from my care.'

'They'll be negative. I'm fine. Just a little overworked, that's all. Now you're here I can sit back and relax a bit more.'

'Doctors always make the worst patients.' He smiled as he dried his hands with paper towel.

At that moment a nurse arrived with a brown manila folder. 'Those urgent blood results, Mr Baptiste.' She laid them down on top of the metal sink and walked away.

Sam suddenly felt her blood pressure rise and she grew hot. Her stomach was churning now. They'd be negative, right?

She reached for the folder to read them herself, but she was too slow—Yanis already had them in his grasp. He gave her a look. *Are you ready?*

And then he opened the folder.

CHAPTER THREE

'YOU'RE PREGNANT.'

The words fell from his mouth in disbelief. He'd considered it a possibility, but hoped he was wrong. Now there it was in black and white, and he was stunned.

His past flashed before his eyes. Those moments in Sonography with Giselle. The tears. The pain. The grief. The isolation. The rejection. The accusations.

'What? No. Give me that.'

Sam snatched the slip of paper from his hand and scanned it, frowning as she read everything. The beta HCG numbers, her name, her date of birth, checking it was *her* result and not someone else's.

Yanis watched her silently, his mind whirring with fears and thoughts that he hadn't had for a long time. Sam was most definitely pregnant.

'Is it mine?'

He had to know. Had to know if she'd slept with someone else after him. Had to know whether or not he was going to be let off the hook. Even thinking it, hoping for it, he felt bad. Because even if it wasn't his, Sam was still going to be left pregnant, and he could tell from what he knew of this woman that having a child and being a mother were not part of her life plan.

He could even remember them talking about such things back in Paris. They'd chatted about where they saw themselves in the future. What they wanted to achieve. All Sam had talked about was work. Maybe starting up a clinical trial, with all that entailed, and really putting herself and St Barnabas's on the map as *the* leading neurosurgery centre in the UK.

Were there tears in her eyes? Seeing her look so shocked made him want to comfort her and pull her close, but he just couldn't do it.

Sam glared at him and then stalked past him, blasting the door open with her palm and striding off down the corridor.

She didn't want this either.

He followed quickly. He was not going to allow her to shut him out on this. He needed to know.

He caught up with her by the lifts. 'Sam?'

'We need to run the test again. It's got to be faulty, or it's got mixed up in Pathology.'

'They're your results.'

'Stuff gets mixed up all the time—'

'Sam. Look at me. Is this baby mine?' he said urgently, making her meet his gaze, wanting her to focus, but not wanting to cause a scene in the busy hospital. He needed her to accept what was printed on that slip. There'd been no mistake and he was not going to waste time by pretending that there had. Facts needed clarifying.

The lift doors pinged open and she stepped inside. He went with her. 'I need you to answer me.'

'I didn't sleep with anyone else!'

Yanis sucked in a breath. So it *was* his. She was pregnant with his child. They'd slept together three months ago—that meant she'd had no antenatal care in that time. They had no idea if this baby was healthy. And with *his* history he needed to know and he needed to know now.

'We need to organise an ultrasound. Right now.'

Sam shook her head. 'No.'

By God, this woman was stubborn! 'We need to check on the baby!'

'I don't want to see it! If I see it, it'll be real, and then—'

'It *is* real! You cannot stick your head in the sand on this one, *mon amie*!'

The lift opened at the neurology floor and Sam gave him one last withering look before stalking out of it. She headed to the main desk, where she took a seat and angrily punched her password and code into the hospital computer. She started to write up her part of the surgical notes on Max. Then she paused, her hands over the keyboard stopped, trembled, and her whole body sagged.

He couldn't see her face. Her long auburn locks hid it from view. But by the shake of her shoulders he knew she was crying.

He had done this to her. And she didn't know the worst of it yet. His heart ached for her. He was wishing he could protect her from all that was to come. He'd never wanted this to happen. Not again. And to think that he could be about to put Sam, of all people, through something so terrifying...

'*Ma chérie...*'

He reached out and tucked her hair behind her ear, draped his arm around her shoulder. She leaned into him and he wrapped both arms around her, just held her for a minute.

She didn't seem to mind that someone might see her crying, but knowing how sad she'd been after losing Emmeline, back in Paris, he wondered if the staff here were maybe used to her getting upset after losing a patient, and that was what they thought this was?

A nurse who passed them by silently mouthed *Is she okay?* He gave a quick nod to indicate that he had this, and that Sam was fine and she could carry on with her job.

It was nice that the staff here looked out for one another. That was the best thing about working in healthcare. Everyone usually had each other's backs. They were a family.

But as he held Sam in his arms, he wondered how much hurt he might put her through. She didn't know what had happened between him and his ex-wife, Giselle, and he knew that at some point he would have to tell her. Warn her. Yet now was not the time. He knew he had to let Sam accept the fact that she was pregnant first. And until they got a scan to see exactly how healthy this baby was, there was no point in worrying her unduly.

On the desk was a box of extra-large tissues, and he reached for one and passed it to her. 'Dry your eyes.'

She wiped at her eyes and sniffed. 'Thank you.'

'For what?'

'For not freaking out on me.'

He smiled. 'That's okay. You were freaking out enough for both of us. If I'd got involved with that, too, we both might have been sent to the fourth floor.'

The fourth floor was Psychiatry.

Sam hiccupped a laugh and let out a long breath. 'What are we going to do?'

Yanis sighed, glad that she was now co-operating. Asking for his advice. He knew how much it must be taking her to rely on someone else. The woman he'd known in Paris had been a tour de force and had relied on *no one.*

'We're going to get information. Organise an ultrasound. Get your dates. Measurements. Make sure that *bébé et maman* are both okay.'

She looked at him then, seemed reassured by his kindness. 'At least one of us knows how to behave,' she said. 'And this baby will need it. Because I don't have a single clue on how to be a good *maman.*'

He smiled again, his eyes full of affection. 'I'll buy you a manual.'

Sam was a woman who could endure surgeries lasting an entire day. She had the patience to endure complicated and delicate operations, knowing that at times she would have to work at a snail's pace, so as not to do harm to any important areas of a patient's brain as she worked to remove tumours and clots or clip aneurysms. She could sit by a patient's bedside, waiting for them to wake, and not mind if it took hours, but this forty-minute wait she was having to endure for

an ultrasound scan of her womb seemed in-
terminable.

'Why are they taking so long?'

'It's a busy clinic. And don't forget we've
not done this like all the other women here,
who saw their family doctor first. We've
used the privilege of being colleagues and
they've fitted us in. We should be patient.'

'I'm not sure I know how.'

Becoming the patient and sitting in a hospital waiting room was terribly familiar to
Sam, and it was bringing back memories
that she had tried to forget many years ago.
Of course, back then, she had been much
smaller, and she'd not had a handsome man
by her side but her mother, who would sit
there reminding her quietly about what to
say and what *not* to say.

That had been easy enough. Sometimes
she'd felt so ill it had been simple to stay
quiet and let her mother act the part of a dis-
traught parent who *'just knew'* something
was *'terribly wrong'* with her daughter. She
would let them prod her, poke her with needles, examine her wherever her mother had
said there was a problem, because she herself

had wanted to feel better, and she'd known that the doctors had the power to make that happen.

In a way, she had been in awe of them, and it was where her own love of medicine had come from. Its seeming ability to make miracles happen. But she'd also known, from all the times before, that even if she got better she would fall ill again soon after, and sometimes the treatment would hurt. Sometimes she would be left in pain.

Technically, she knew this was not the same. She was not about to be used like a human guinea pig. This was a simple ultrasound. It would not hurt. If anything, it would be slightly uncomfortable as they pressed down upon her full bladder—they'd asked her to turn up with one. And this scan would give them the answers both she and Yanis needed.

But as she looked around the room at all the women, some with bumps that were barely there and others full and wholesome, with rounded, swollen abdomens, she couldn't help but imagine what that might be like. Becoming a mother...

Mothers were supposed to be loving and kind. They were supposed to be a child's soft place to fall. But Sam was convinced she could never be that. Surely she was all hard, sharp edges? Her broken pieces mangled together with the glue of time?

I simply don't know how to do this. What if I can't? What then? Do I fail this child? Doom it to years of therapy?

She shifted in her seat at the discomfort of her thoughts.

Yanis turned to look at her and she gave him a reassuring smile, but she was feeling anything but. His life was changing, too. This wasn't all about her. How was *he* feeling about this? He hadn't said much.

'What are you thinking?' she asked.

He shook his head. 'I don't know.'

'This must be as much of a shock to you as it is to me.'

He smiled. 'It certainly is.'

'It's going to mean us both having time off and parental leave. That's going to be really challenging.'

'We'll work something out.'

'I'm not giving up work. What I do is my

life. It's what I live for,' she said, making sure he understood that she was not going to become a stay-at-home mother.

Neurology *was* what she lived for! It was all she'd ever lived for. She'd always been fascinated by medicine, and had known she would become a doctor, but specialising in neurology was her passion. It had been ever since her mother, and then her doctors, had suspected she had a brain tumour as a child.

The idea of someone working in her head... Sam had begun doing her own research. That had been hard back then—there hadn't been any books on neurology in her school library, and when she'd asked the librarian to order some... Well, she'd got a few strange looks. But the workings of the brain had fascinated her. And had gone on doing so for most of her adult life.

It was one of the largest and most complex organs of the human body. It contained over a hundred billion nerves and created trillions of connections every day through the synapses. It was who you were. How you reacted to things. How you loved. What made you laugh and cry. It was where the emotions came from, where memories were stored.

To think that all that passion for her job might fade, that this pregnancy was about to sideswipe everything she knew...

It was terrifying.

'I don't think I can do this, Yanis.'

He turned to look at her. 'You can.'

'How do you know? You don't really know me... You don't know anything about me! We're colleagues, thrown together by circumstance. I don't think you want this either—this *situation*.'

He sighed. 'It's certainly a surprise. But if we can excise tumours and clip bleeds and bring people back from the brink of death or a lifetime of disability, then I think we can do this, too. Millions of people worldwide do it, and they all do so without formal training. We're intelligent. Capable. I believe in us.'

She was envious of his certainty. Where did it come from? She wanted to believe his words. They made sense—of course they did. But her fear was impinging on every thought she had. What if she failed? What if she ruined this child's life the way her mother had almost ruined hers? Sam always tried to be the best she could be in anything. In her job. As a friend. Could she be a brilliant mother?

Her fear and her doubt told her no.

'Samantha Gordon?'

A lady dressed in pink scrubs stood in the doorway with a clipboard.

Sam and Yanis glanced at one another and he reached for her hand, giving it a quick squeeze.

'We can do this.'

She gave him an uncertain look and allowed him to lead her by the hand into the darkened room.

The sonographer introduced herself as Marta. 'You can take a seat on the bed, Ms Gordon.'

'Thank you for fitting us in. We both appreciate this very much,' Yanis said.

He felt it was important to say that. To show gratitude. It had been a long time since he'd been in an ultrasound room like this one and he could feel his apprehension growing.

Rooms like this either brought brilliant news or horrendously bad news. There never seemed to be any in between, as far as he was concerned. His last visit to a room like this had been with Giselle, his ex-wife, and the news then had been devastating. Their son's heart had stopped beating at thirty weeks' gestation.

Showing a little gratitude might win him some good luck points. It was worth a try.

'I just need to ask you a few basic questions,' said Marta, and ran Sam through them.

She wanted to know when her last period was, whether she had a regular cycle, her GP details, her medical history. All standard stuff. But he could hear the nervousness in Sam's voice as she responded and he put what he hoped was a soothing arm around her shoulders as he watched her fiddle with the blue sanitary paper that covered the bed.

She glanced up at him and gave him a brief, grateful smile. He saw fear in her soft blue eyes. A need to be protected. He wished he could protect her from everything, but that was not a power he had. Instead, he gave her another little squeeze, wanting her to know that they were in this together for the baby's sake, if no one else's.

'All right—so if you could lie back for me? That's it.' Marta tucked some more of the blue paper into the top of Sam's underwear. 'And this will feel cold.'

She squirted gel onto her belly and he watched her flinch. She gave him a look of such sheer terror that he reached out and took her hand.

'It's going to be okay.'

He had no true way of knowing, of course, but he felt it was important to say it. That she should hear it. And, no matter what the health of the baby, he wanted her to know that he would help her through whatever was to come. He would not abandon her. That was not the type of man he was.

He had supported Giselle as much as he could, but at the end of the day, even he hadn't been able to help, and they had separated. It was something that had made him feel a failure for such a long time and the reason why his work had become so important. At work, he could help. He could make a difference. He could control things.

This was not an area in which he had any control. Nor did Sam. So he knew how she felt in this moment.

Marta placed the probe on Sam's abdomen and began to move it around. Neither he nor Sam could see the screen. The sonographer had it turned in her direction only. He knew they all did this to check everything was all right before they turned the screen to show the ecstatic parents-to-be. It was a shield until it was a gift.

Her face gave nothing away as she moved the probe.

'It's bad news, isn't it? It's okay, you can tell me. It's a chemical pregnancy? A molar pregnancy?' Sam asked.

He was surprised that she was already assuming it was going to be bad news. He'd thought he was the only one. But then, she was a realist, and he liked that about her. There were no fluffy rainbows and unicorns in Sam's life—just cold, hard facts. Maybe that would help them deal with whatever was to come.

At that point Marta shook her head, then smiled. 'Is there any history of multiple pregnancy on either side?' she asked, and turned the screen.

Yanis's mouth went dry as he stared at the image. Was he seeing right? Was he reading this correctly?

'Twins?'

Two babies. They were having *two babies*. Two!

He squeezed Sam's hand tighter and she looked at him in shock.

'What? Twins? No, it can't be!'

'It can and it is.' Marta smiled some more as she showed them in detail. Baby A, and then she morphed the image to Baby B. 'And they're both good sizes, too, according to these measurements.'

Yanis almost didn't know what to say. Was this really happening? Everything he'd been through...everything he'd lost... His dream of starting a family had been torn from his tight grasp and destroyed—was it suddenly a possibility again? It almost didn't seem real.

His initial feelings of surprise and joy suddenly dived down into the deep, dark pits of fear. This could all still go horribly wrong. Was he about to send Samantha through something he never wanted to see a woman he cared for go through again? There wasn't just the risk of losing one baby here—there was the risk of losing *two*.

'Want to hear the heartbeats?'

Marta pressed a button and there it was. Two healthy heartbeats—*pow, pow, pow*—thudding rhythmically through the room. They sounded strong. They sounded steady. Exactly as they should be.

But then, that was how it had been with his son. He'd seemed healthy. Nothing wrong on the scans. He'd simply died in utero. Just as he and Giselle had been beginning to believe that they were on the home stretch. That everything was fine...that *this time* they could start decorating the nursery and buying a cot.

'Twins... I don't believe it...' Sam's voice trembled with awe and shock. 'And they're both healthy? All looks good?'

Marta nodded. 'At the moment. They're sharing a sac, so they're identical twins. They're also sharing a placenta and blood flow, so we'll need to keep an eye on that.'

'TTTS. Right...' Sam nodded, sounding

more sure, for some strange reason, now that she was talking about something grim.

TTTS stood for Twin-to-Twin Transfusion Syndrome. In a twin pregnancy, abnormal blood vessels could form in the placenta, allowing blood to flow unevenly between the two babies, causing one to get too much and the other to get too little. It could make them very sick, and in some cases it could be fatal.

'Your placenta is quite low at the moment, though that could change. As the uterus grows with the pregnancy, it can move higher up and not cause a problem.'

'You're talking about the risk of placenta praevia?' Sam said.

It was a condition that could cause severe bleeding and lead to a medical emergency during the pregnancy or at delivery.

'We'll monitor you regularly.'

'Right.'

Again, he thought how Sam sounded strangely okay about the risk of these complications. As if she'd expected it. Was it because it grounded her? Didn't allow her to get overwhelmed by the *'twin'* news in all of this?

Because all Yanis heard was *Risk. Danger. Complications.* Real reasons as to why this pregnancy might not be successful. He blamed himself. But he could not let it show for Sam. She would need him to be strong for her, the way he had tried to be strong for Giselle.

'Would you like pictures?' Marta asked, the bright smile back upon her face.

Sam nodded and let out a heavy breath. She looked up at him. 'Yanis? You okay?'

He forced a smile. 'I'm good,' he lied, feeling sick with fear.

Back in the lift going up to Neurology, Sam continued to stare at and study the ultrasound photos she held in her hand. It felt a little unreal, but there they were. Two babies. And they were in her womb, growing like weeds.

What a day this had been.

She rubbed at her abdomen, as if making a physical connection between the scan pictures and her body. Twins… And she had the risk of placenta praevia and twin-to-twin transfusion syndrome. Of course she did. She wasn't surprised about that at all.

'What do we do now?' she asked Yanis.

Yanis looked as if he was in another world, and it was strange to see him like that. Usually he was the quintessential confident Frenchman. Stunning to look at, as always. But now he looked as if he wasn't present. As if he were somewhere else. He certainly didn't look happy.

'It's a bit of an odd situation we find ourselves in and this is a surprise to me,' she said. 'So God only knows what you must be feeling. A quick hook-up with a colleague and wham, bam, thank you, Sam—it's *twins.*'

She folded the pictures and slid them into the chest pocket of her scrubs. No point in telling her colleagues until she was ready.

She sighed. 'If you want to bow out, that's fine. I'm wishing I could do that myself.'

The lift doors opened and they stepped out into the corridor.

He met her gaze then. 'What are you saying?'

His quick, sharp reaction surprised her. 'I don't know! I don't *know* what I'm saying. All I know is that I find myself in an impossible situation and my brain is telling me that

I can't do this. Be a mother, that is. I don't know how.'

'Of course you can. Anyone can,' he said irritably.

'Anyone?' she scoffed. 'You should meet some of the parents I see in A & E. Some of them don't have a clue.'

'You do. You're intelligent. A doctor.'

'Yes, well, sometimes too much knowledge can be a bad thing.'

She thought of her own mother and her extensive knowledge. Thought of all the medical books her mother had pored over at home. The second-hand textbooks on medicine and physiology she'd managed to score, almost as if the books themselves were drugs. They had been her mother's heroin. Her cocaine. Her addiction. They'd meant more to her than her own daughter. And she'd used them to create the situations she'd craved and needed. She'd deliberately harmed Sam, so that she would receive the attention she craved from doctors and the nurses and consultants.

It had been something she'd thrived on. Something that had put Sam in harm's way. Sam believed it had begun years before, though. That craving for attention. When her mother had fallen pregnant with her and her father had left her, not wanting to be a parent. It had been triggered then.

How could Sam be sure she wouldn't be the same way? Look at her own medical knowledge! It was hard enough looking after one baby, but two... Think of the stress! What if she snapped? What if she couldn't do it?

All of this and more flooded through her brain in an instant, but she let none of it show on her face.

'I just... I just don't know if I can do this. Finding out I'm having one baby is stressful enough, but twins...'

'I know it's hard, but let's not have any jerk-knee reactions.'

'It's knee-jerk. And you still haven't told me how you feel about all of this.'

He pushed himself away from the wall and ran his hands through his hair. It sprang perfectly back into place and she found herself inordinately annoyed by that small thing, wishing her own hair behaved as impeccably. But then she realised she was allowing herself to be distracted from the elephant in the room. Which, as it turned out, was *her*.

'I think… I think we take this day by day,' he said.

She nodded. 'You mean ignore it until we have no choice? Seems like a good plan. Except the sonographer made it clear that this is a risky pregnancy and will most likely go very wrong indeed. One baby could become a giant leech. The other will be tiny—like Alice when she took the *Drink Me* potion. Or, hey, I could bleed out at any point! Won't that be fun! Perhaps we should take notice of it then?'

She realised even as she said it that her hysterical sarcasm probably wasn't the best response, but she couldn't help herself. It was easy enough for him to say they should take it day by day, but he wasn't the one growing new life! Two new lives! He wasn't the one who would have to face the medical issues, the doctors looking her over as if she was some strange specimen, poking and prodding her, sticking needles in her, doing internal examinations. She was the one who would have to give birth. Twice!

Sam didn't want to feel bitter, but this situation seemed grossly outweighed in Yanis's favour. Not hers. He wouldn't have to watch and feel his body change. He wouldn't have to go through cravings or bloating or cramps. Or stretch marks or heartburn or labour. This was *easy* for him.

He might say that they were in this together, but were they? She had no proof of that. He could walk away at any time. She would always be the one left holding the baby.

The *babies*! Plural!

'That's not fair,' he said.

'Nothing about this is fair!' she argued, turning away from him.

At that moment her pager went off, distracting her from her upset, pulling her back into her other world, in which she was a highly respected neurosurgeon and she was *needed*.

'My next patient is being prepped. I've got to go.'

'What is it?' he asked.

'Private patient. He's got a benign tumour

impinging on his spine and affecting leg movement.'

'I'm free. Let me assist you in Theatre.'

'I don't need you babysitting me, Yanis. I'm fine.'

'I'm sure you are. But it's always good to have an extra pair of hands. And you've had a shock today.'

'So have you,' she challenged.

Lewis Kozalski was an internationally ac-claimed canoeist, who had first noticed a problem with his back and legs after a twenty-four-hour canoe race he'd done for charity. At first he'd put his problems down to having been in the canoe for such a long time, but when the problems had persisted beyond a reasonable time, he'd begun to worry.

'There's this thing we do called a roll,' he explained to Yanis now. 'I was teaching a class of students in a swimming pool, and when I went under the water I didn't have enough strength to roll up again. The pain in my back was horrendous. I had to undo the canoe skirt so that I could get out, and for a minute there I thought I was going to drown.'

'Must have been scary,' Yanis said.

'Not as scary as this.' Lewis was on the bed, waiting for Anaesthesia to do their thing.

'You're in excellent hands. Ms Gordon is very confident that she can excise this tumour.'

Lewis nodded. 'I hope so.'

'You ready?'

'Yes.'

Yanis gave a quick nod of his head to the anaesthesia team and they got to work, putting Lewis under. He then went to scrub in and found Sam fastening the back of her scrub cap.

'He's nervous,' he told her.

'Aren't we all?'

'You're not nervous about this surgery?'

She smiled. 'No. In this, I know *exactly* what I'm doing.'

'Good. And you've had something to eat?'

She began to scrub. 'I'm not going to faint, Yanis. Relax.'

'I'm allowed to worry.'

'Are you?'

'I think so. Besides, last time I could catch you. This time I'll be on the opposite side of the table, so if you go down you're going to hit the floor hard.'

'It's never going to happen.'

'Good.'

'But it's nice to know you care, I guess.'

'I do.'

She smiled. 'The twins thing hasn't scared you off? You sure you don't want to run? I wouldn't blame you. In fact, I think I'd understand it.'

Yanis turned on his own faucet and began to scrub. 'Because you want to run?'

'Yes. But it's hard to run from your own body, so I'm kinda stuck with it.'

'Whatever this pregnancy throws at us, I'm sure we'll be able to handle it.'

'You don't sound sure.'

No, he didn't. He'd only said it out loud as a way to convince himself.

When did he tell her? When did he tell her that Giselle hadn't lost one pregnancy, but three?

Sam already seemed to be expecting the worst. The warning today about the risk of TTTS was bad enough. What had *he* passed on to their babies? Were there genetic errors in his make-up that determined every pregnancy he fathered wouldn't last? If this pregnancy didn't make it, would Sam blame herself, or him? And if she did blame him, would he be able to cope with it?

He'd told himself after Giselle that he would never try for a family ever again. It was too risky. Too heartbreaking when your every hope and dream dissolved into cramps and clots.

He could hardly believe that only a few days ago he'd been so excited for this new start in Richmond. Thrilled to find that Sam was still there, believing that the two of them could help make Barney's neurosurgical centre one of the leading lights in UK medicine. And now this?

He liked Sam. He more than liked Sam. That night they'd spent together had been magical, and he'd felt a connection with her he'd not felt for a long time. He'd hoped for friendship, for fun and laughter and joyful times. Instead, he was going to put a woman he cared for through the most difficult time of her life.

He'd tried so hard to be there for Giselle, but he'd needed someone to be there for *him*. And although his family had tried to understand, none of them had truly known how he felt. His brothers and sisters had had their own family without a single problem. How could they know how he'd felt? How hopeless…helpless.

No matter what he'd said or done, none of it had seemed to make anything better for Giselle. He hadn't been able to take away her pain, or his own. The idea that he might have to go through all that heartbreak again was just too horrible for words.

They both walked through into Theatre and the scrub nurses helped them on with their gowns and gloves.

'Let's run it,' said Sam.

The scrub nurse went through Lewis's details and his exact surgery. He watched Sam examine the scan images one last time. She muttered something under her face mask, then said out loud, 'Let's make a difference, everyone. Scalpel.'

Let's make a difference.

He pondered those words. He'd heard her say them in Paris and thought it was just part of her ritual. But now he realised they were proactive. Not reactive. They suggested that the team were doing something to force a positive change.

Maybe he could learn something from that? Maybe he should stop fearing the worst and waiting for something bad to happen and instead imagine only the good—assume that only good would come from this situation he and Sam found themselves in?

He would make sure she accessed all the right healthcare, make sure she took good care of herself, eating and resting properly, and make sure that he was there to support her, to show her that he was an active partner in all of this and that they weren't helpless in this situation.

He could make a difference.

He could show her that they could do this scary thing. Show her that they could support one another and be there for one another and, most importantly, that they could get on with their lives and stop feeling as if they were in a canoe, being hopelessly propelled through some rapids.

They could weather this. They had oars. They could steer, they could take back control, manoeuvre themselves out of the rough water and into the calm. Maybe even get their feet back on dry land.

Okay, their lives were changing even now, but it didn't mean that they were only passive witnesses to it all. They could tackle their fears and their doubts by taking back control. By making a difference to their thought patterns, they could show this pregnancy who was boss and refuse to cower in fear.

Sam made the first cut, and the focus in her gaze made Yanis feel a little better about his decision. He allowed all his previous worries to disappear as the surgery began. What mattered right now was this man on the table. His spine. His tumour. His future. If Sam could push the turmoil of her life to one side and focus, then so could he. He could learn something from her.

He took a deep breath and concentrated.

The rest of the world and all its associated concerns soon melted away.

This was why he loved surgery so much.

CHAPTER FOUR

THE ATRIUM WAS such a calm, soothing place. Real trees, bushes and flowers grew there, in what felt like a tropical glasshouse. The walkways twisted and turned, providing small pockets of privacy, and it was dotted with benches and water features. In the largest of these, koi carp swam serenely beneath the water. It was a good place to think. A perfect place to try to clear your head.

Sam sat there now, staring at the fish in the water, almost hypnotised by their movements.

'Earth to Sam.'

The voice brought her back to the present and she looked up to see her good friend Gil Alexander, the head of neuro rehabilitation. Sam smiled and patted the bench beside her.

Gil sat down. 'You okay? You looked miles away.'

Sam let out a sigh and gave a cynical laugh. 'I'm not and I was.'

'Oh. Anything I can help with?'

She looked at him and shook her head. 'I don't think this is your area of expertise.'

He frowned. 'So it's nothing to do with work, then? Hmm… Interesting. Do you finally have a personal life? What's that like?'

She smiled. It was a long-running joke between them. 'Complicated,' she said.

She'd first met Gil at the hospital, but not as a colleague. Sam had been called down to the emergency department to consult on a patient. She'd done her consult and was just dropping off some paperwork into the tray by the receptionist when she'd spotted him, sitting on a chair in the waiting room, squinting, talking nonsense, obviously waiting to be seen.

Sam had laid a hand on the receptionist's shoulder and asked, 'What's his story?'

The receptionist had shrugged. 'Oh, I don't think he's checked in yet.'

'He's not been triaged? You're sure?'

'I'd have remembered him coming to the desk.'

Sam had known something wasn't right, so she'd gone right out there and knelt in front of him to ask a few questions. His confused answers had concerned her, and after performing a FAST stroke test, which had been negative, she'd felt sure she was dealing with a brain injury. Then he'd seemed to indicate that his head was hurting him intensely, and she'd sent him for a scan and discovered he had a slow brain bleed and needed emergency surgery.

He'd been her first 'catch', and Elliot had been so impressed he'd allowed her to assist in Theatre. Afterwards, he'd been able to tell her what had happened. Gil had had a nasty collision with some other players during a rugby scrum, and although he'd thought at the time he maybe had a mild concussion, he'd rashly assumed he was fine. Though as the day had worn on, he'd begun to feel awful, and that day had somehow made his way to hospital.

The surgery had changed Gil's life, and though he'd been an A & E doctor, he'd changed careers after going through rehabilitation and physiotherapy. He'd retrained and now he ran the neurological rehabilitation centre at Barney's, helping to look after many of her patients. Helping them readjust to life after traumatic brain injury.

'Do tell,' he said now. 'You never know—I might have some wise words.'

Sam let out another sigh. 'You know I went to Paris a few months ago, for that work exchange?'

Gil nodded, sipping from his coffee cup.

'I kind of met someone.'

He raised an eyebrow. 'You didn't say anything when you got back.'

'No... Well, I thought it was nothing.'

'Only it was *something*?'

'Yeah.' She gave another sigh. 'He consoled me after we lost a patient on my last day. A young girl.'

'I'm sorry.'

'I felt so bad... I knew that the girl was scared of the surgery, even though she'd had counselling.'

Gil knew of Sam's past. He'd understand how much that would have hurt.

'I'm sure you did it for the right reasons,' he said.

'Yeah, well… Yanis and I ended up sleeping together.'

When Gil said nothing, she knew she had to say more. If there was anyone on this planet she trusted as a friend, it was Gil. She knew he wouldn't spill her secrets. The friendship they had struck up after his surgery was strong. She was proud of her first catch, her first save, and he was grateful to her for changing his life and making him rethink what he wanted from it.

Medicine could cure, but it could also impact on doctors' lives to such a degree that they had no life outside of the job. It was something that they'd both been guilty of. Only Gil had changed, whereas for Sam, Gil's surgery had just made her even more sure that this was the life she wanted. She was dedicated to her work. Driven by her passion to help save lives.

'And now he's here,' she said. 'Yanis Baptiste?'

Gil nodded. 'I've seen his name on a couple of patient charts. And a few nurses might have drooled over him at break time. Apparently he's *"a looker".* Gil raised his hands to make air quotes and smiled.

Sam laughed. 'He is what they call "easy on the eye".'

'And I assume he wants to carry on the relationship you started back in Paris?'

'Not exactly.'

'Then what?'

Sam sucked in a big breath and then let it out again, biting her lip, grimacing. She turned to him and whispered, 'I'm pregnant.'

And then Gil proved exactly why he was her friend. He didn't let out a low whistle, he didn't laugh, and he didn't smile or offer forced congratulations. He looked directly in her eyes and got straight to the point.

'And how do you feel about that?'

He was such a good man. Empathetic. Kind. She hoped he'd find someone to be with one day. He deserved to have that.

'I'm terrified.'

He reached out and laid his hand on hers, before squeezing her fingers. 'Which bit scares you the most?'

'All of it.'

'Motherhood?'

She nodded and wiped away a tear.

'You won't turn out like her. You're different. You're not the same person.'

'Children deserve the best parents, Gil. Parents who love one another. Parents who are there for each other. We barely know each other. We had one night and now this. And it's hard enough looking after one child, but two…'

'It's twins?'

'Yeah.'

He was silent for a moment, looking out across the atrium, waiting for a couple of patients to pass, dragging their IV poles behind them. When they were alone again, he said, 'I'm not going to lie: parenting will be hard. And you're being thrown in at the deep end. Will this Mr Baptiste be there to help you?'

'He says he will. I think so.'

'You need to make sure.'

'But what if it all goes wrong? A twin pregnancy is a risky one, and my body hasn't exactly done the right thing in the past.'

'There's nothing wrong with your body. Not now. You're strong. Any faults it had previously were deliberately put there by your mother.'

'But when you're told that you're broken *every single day...*'

'You're not broken. Look at you. You fix things. You're one of the top neurosurgeons in the country. When were you ill last? That cold last summer? Everybody gets those. There's no reason why you can't continue in this pregnancy and do so without a single issue rearing its ugly head.'

'I knew you'd talk some sense into me.'

'I like getting to save *you* occasionally. You brought me back from the brink—it's only fair you let me think I'm doing the same for you.' Gil smiled.

'Thanks...' said Sam. 'I best be getting back. I've got an outpatient clinic list to get through. Are you okay? Everything fine with you?'

'Don't you worry about me. I'm good.'

'Okay.' She dropped her hand on his shoulder as a physical thank-you, and then headed off back into the hospital.

Gil was right. She needed to think positively. It had been proved in many research papers that having a positive mindset could be very beneficial to overall health, and if there was anything she could do to make this pregnancy go well then she ought to do it.

This wasn't just about her any more.

She had a family to think of.

'I thought you'd like to know that Lewis is doing well.'

Yanis popped his head around Sam's door just before she started her outpatient clinic. He'd checked on her patient in the ICU and, although it was early days, Lewis seemed to have homeostasis—was maintaining his blood pressure, temperature and respirations within normal parameters.

The first twenty-four hours after surgery were always crucial. Anything could happen. The body might throw a clot from the surgery, there could be a fluid build-up at the operative site, a drainage tube could block, or an infection could set in. Patients were closely monitored whether they were private, like Lewis, or not.

'Good. Thanks for letting me know,' Sam said. 'Is he on half-hourly obs?'

'*Oui.*'

'That's good.'

She smiled at him then, as if she wasn't sure of what to say next, so he slipped into her room and closed the door behind him, before walking over to her desk and sitting on the chair across from her.

'I want you to feel that you can come to me at any time,' he said.

'All right…'

'I feel that this is something that we should be able to get through by relying on one another.'

'Okay… Though I might have difficulties with that. I've never relied on anyone in my entire life. That's going to be strange for me—just so you know.'

He smiled. 'Strange is okay. Impossible I would have a problem with.'

Sam nodded. 'Noted. Anything else?'

'*Oui.* Let me take you out to dinner.'

'Dinner? Why?'

'Because we need to eat—and why not do that with each other, to help build our bond?'

'You want to build our bond?' she asked uncertainly.

'Don't you? We're going to have children together.'

'Dinner. Right. Okay. What time?'

'I could pick you up at seven?'

She smiled. 'You could.'

'I would need your address.'

She reached for a notepad and scribbled her details down on it, then passed it over, her cheeks flushed with heat. 'It's a date.'

Now it was his turn to look at her intensely. 'It most certainly is.'

Sam was struggling. She didn't normally do *dates*.

Dates involved getting to know people and placing your trust in them. She wasn't able to do that easily, so whenever she felt like male company, she'd sort out the convenient kind that involved a quick tussle under the bedsheets and leave it at that. No getting to know one another. No finding out what their favourite breakfast cereal was or whether they preferred cats to dogs. It was all about scratching a physical itch and then moving on.

She hadn't done it often. Why would she

when it meant exposing herself to scrutiny? Showing someone her scars? To them they might mean nothing, but to her they were glowing beacons that revealed how much she'd let someone else control her.

Those days were over. She was her own person and she'd got used to only having herself to look after. It was easy. Less chance of screwing up. Less chance of losing control.

But dating...? That was a different kettle of fish.

Her last real date had been her prom date, and she'd chosen someone who'd been no physical threat to her whatsoever—a geeky young man who had been very Clark Kent and president of the chess club. He'd turned up at her aunt's house and presented her with a corsage, and that was as far as their physical contact had gone.

So why had she agreed to this?

Because he caught me off guard. Because I didn't know what else to say. Because... Because I'm curious and getting to know Yanis seems like a sensible thing to do.

A sensible thing. Gil had suggested that

they would do a better job if they supported one another and that made sense. Why fight it?

She kept telling herself, as she curled her hair with curling tongs and put on make-up, that it had absolutely *nothing* to do with the fact that she still felt incredibly attracted to the man, and absolutely *everything* to do with her trying to hold out an olive branch and become a sensible adult.

In simple terms, they were going to have to parent together. Which meant, if they were going to do it right, they would need good communication. And that meant actually liking the guy and getting on with him. So if they needed to go out to dinner to do that then she would give it a go. For the babies' sakes.

She still couldn't quite believe it! Twins... It was crazy...

On the dot of seven, her doorbell rang. Her stomach felt like a knot of nerves, but she sucked in a deep breath, headed for the front door and opened it.

Yanis looked incredible. The kind of incredible that made her ovaries ache and her heart pound.

She was amazed she was having such a reaction.

I mean, he wears a shirt and tie to work, for God's sake.

But without the addition of stethoscope and ID lanyard, he looked a different kind of edible.

Dark trousers moulded his strong legs, and a fitted navy shirt emphasised the bright blue of his eyes, the narrowness of his waist and the broadness of his shoulders. And what was that scent he wore? She wanted to just stand there for a moment, close her eyes and breathe him in, allow the aroma to caress her senses and make her go all warm and gooey inside.

'Wow. You look…nice.'

Yanis smiled. *'Et tu as l'air belle.'*

She tried to dredge up her secondary school French. *And you have…something-something…*

She must have frowned, because he translated for her. 'And you look beautiful.'

'Oh.' She blushed, hoping she was blushing

in a pretty kind of way, and not in a blotchy I'm-having-a-hot-flush kind of way. 'Thanks. Where are we going?'

'To Le Chef.'

'French food? Sounds great. Let me just grab my bag.'

She slipped it off the back of a chair, placed her keys and mobile phone inside, and then set off down the path towards his car. She could feel the light touch of his fingers on the small of her back and it reminded her of the last time his fingers had touched her that night in Paris.

She felt herself grow hot, and was glad that he didn't know what she was thinking about. She'd spent many a night since Paris thinking about that encounter, wishing she was someone else so that she could go back to him again and again. He was a skilled lover— someone who knew what he was doing and knew how to pleasure a woman.

How many lovers had he had? Looking the way he did, she had to assume that he'd had many. Was she just one of many notches on his bedpost? Did he resent her for trapping him into fatherhood? He wasn't acting as if he was, but could anyone say they truly knew one another? He wore no ring, and she knew nothing of his past, though she did recall hearing something about the ending of a long-term relationship that he'd been involved in. Had he celebrated his freedom from that with multiple lovers? Most men would. Wouldn't they?

As Yanis drove them to the restaurant, she was trying her best to think of something casual to say. It was easy at work, because they could discuss their patients, but in this instance, what sort of things did people talk about? She knew she wasn't skilled in this arena, and they had so much riding on them getting this relationship right—even if it was just a parenting one. She was terrified of screwing it up.

Hey, kids...well, yes, I did know your father, but I said something really stupid and now you'll never see him ever again. Soz.

'So, what do you think of Richmond? How does it compare to Paris?'

Yanis smiled. 'They cannot be compared. Paris is Paris. It holds a certain style and *feel*. It has a beating heart that no other place has.

Richmond is quiet, compared to my home city. Greener. I like Richmond Park. I go running there most mornings.'

'You run?'

She tried to imagine him in tee shirt and shorts, his powerful leg muscles flexing and burning, sweat running down his forehead, darkening his tee. Yanis in the shower afterwards, naked and hot…

She cleared her throat.

'I try to,' he said. 'Do you run?'

'Me? No. I do the occasional spin class when I feel I ought to be doing more exercise, but I figure I walk enough miles when I'm at work, so…'

'You should come running with me sometime.'

'In my condition?' She laughed.

'Maybe afterwards, then.'

Afterwards.

After the pregnancy.

So he *was* thinking of sticking around for a while, then. The idea of having Yanis Baptiste in her life for ever was…disconcerting. Nice, but strange. What would they be to one another? Two people who just happened to co-parent? Or something more? Friends with benefits? Until Yanis found someone better?

Even though Sam was aware that to some people she was a great catch, in herself she knew that she wouldn't be able to persuade herself that she had anything she could offer another person. Not like that. Not long term. Long-term relationships meant give and take, trust and respect, and though she could do all those things, her distrust of people ran deep.

Her own mother—the woman who was meant to have loved her and protected her to the ends of the earth—had been the one to harm her and hurt her, the most. If her own mother could do that, what might someone else do? Someone who didn't have that familial connection?

Yanis seemed great. Of course he did. He was handsome and intelligent and caring. But what lurked beneath the surface? Who was the real Yanis?

'Maybe,' she said.

'You could be one of those mothers who runs whilst pushing those off-road strollers I keep seeing.'

'Or you could be one of those fathers who push the stroller,' she countered.

He nodded and laughed gently. 'I could. You see? We can do this. Two mature adults… discussing how to parent.'

She didn't know how to answer that. Technically, he was correct. And if they kept it that emotionless and simple then, sure, it wouldn't be a problem. But life wasn't like that, was it? Emotion was wrapped around everything. Every decision you made. Could it be that black and white? She doubted it.

Le Chef had its own small parking area, and Yanis managed to find a spot quite easily. The evening was cool, and she was glad she'd brought a coat. Once again she felt Yanis's hand on the small of her back as they walked in and he confirmed the reservation in his name.

The waiter took them to a nice little table for two, by the terrace, so that they could look out upon the small garden there. It was beautiful. Intimate. A potted garden of bushes and small fruit trees, herbs and flowers, lit by the most gorgeous Victorian-style lamps.

They took their seats and the waiter poured water into both of their glasses.

'This is nice. Have you been here before?' she asked.

'*Non.* But it was on my brother's list of recommendations.'

'Oh. Okay... Is this the brother who tags rhino?'

He smiled. 'Yes.'

'Do you have other family? Any more Baptistes I should know about?'

'My sister Yvette. She is a schoolteacher.'

'And your parents?'

'My father was also a teacher. My mother is a critical care nurse.'

'Is that where your passion for medicine came from?'

'Perhaps. I know I was always fascinated by her stories of life and death. It may have had an impact on my decision making. What about you? What made you choose medicine?'

She didn't feel she could tell him the truth about that yet. She was too ashamed. So she decided to go with a half-truth. 'My mother had a passion for health and medicine, too.

The way she talked about doctors and the nurses, how they made her feel... I wanted to be like them, I guess.'

How could she tell him that she'd wished that she alone could have been enough for her mother? That she alone could have provided her mother with enough love so that she hadn't done what she had? So that her mother hadn't looked to medical professionals to provide her with the attention and care she'd so desperately sought?

She took a sip of her water, just as the waiter brought over the menus. Sam was glad of the distraction and for a moment to hide as she allowed her gaze to travel over the unfamiliar words. Most of it was in French, but thankfully there were English translations underneath each item.

'This all sounds wonderful.'

'Have you told your mother about the pregnancy?'

Sam bit her lip behind the menu. What to say? That she only called her mother once a month? That a lot of their phone calls were harrowing and Sam often had to put the phone down on her? That telling her mother she was going to become a grandmother would make her want to get back into Sam's life and she'd spent years without her in it?

'Not yet.'

'Any reason why?'

'It's just…early days, that's all.'

He looked at her strangely, and she knew what he was thinking. Technically, she was out of the first trimester, so the risk of miscarriage was less, but she was very aware that her pregnancy could have complications—so, no, there was no way she would tell her mother any of that. It would reopen old wounds.

'Have you told *your* family?' she countered, throwing the focus back onto him.

He smiled. *'Oui.'*

'How did they take it?'

'They were surprised, but happy.'

He looked away then, as if he was also only telling a half-truth. So they'd been happy… but what else? Yanis wasn't saying.

Then she realised he was signalling for the waiter.

'Are you ready to order, *monsieur…mademoiselle*?'

Yanis looked back at her then, and she nodded.

'I'll have the potted crab with sourdough toast to start, and the confit duck leg with dauphinoise potatoes for main, please.'

The waiter scribbled her order into his notebook. 'And for you, *monsieur*?'

'The salmon gravadlax to start and the marinated chicken for main, *s'il vous plaît*.'

'Excellent choice. Would you like to see our wine list?'

Yanis looked at Sam.

'I won't, but you have some, if you want.'

'I'm driving. No, thank you,' he said to the waiter.

'We do some excellent mocktails, *monsieur*, if you are looking to avoid alcohol.'

'A Shirley Temple would be nice,' she said.

'Make that two.' Yanis nodded and the waiter bowed and hurried away to fulfil their order.

She liked it that he was talking in English here. It would have been so easy for him to converse with the staff in his native language, but he'd kept to English so that she knew what was being said. It was nice. Considerate.

But she'd already known that about him. Even in Paris, when they'd been surrounded by native French speakers, if she or one of the other English doctors had been there he had automatically spoken in English. She'd been so grateful that he knew her language well, because she certainly couldn't manage the French language, and that had been a real worry for her, going over to Paris for that work exchange.

After their mocktails had been delivered, Sam smiled at Yanis over the table. He really was the most delectable-looking man, and the candlelight made him even more so. It was hard to believe that they were in this situation, but here they were, and she didn't know what she was going to do about the fact that she was still highly attracted to him.

Did he feel the same about her?

Would it be dangerous to add attraction to this situation?

Would it be better to keep their relationship as just friends?

She wasn't sure she had it in her to get

involved in a relationship, because what if they fouled it up before the babies were born? What then? If there was hostility between herself and the father, that wouldn't be good, right? If her body had the capacity to fail her, did she really want her emotional state to screw this up, too?

Their starters arrived, looking delicious.

'Bon appetit.' The waiter smiled and then made himself scarce.

Sam knew she needed to keep herself and Yanis as friends. That she knew she could do. They'd done it in Paris. Why not here in Richmond and at Barney's, too?

She tucked in, feeling ravenous despite her nerves. Something weird had happened since the discovery of her pregnancy. It was as if now it was official, and she *knew*, her body was letting her know in no uncertain terms what it wanted—and that was plenty of food. As a surgeon, she often went without food or drink for hours, especially if she had a busy clinic or was operating, and this new territory was making her wonder if she'd be able to get through those ten-hour, twelve-hour, twenty-hour surgeries without stopping to refuel halfway through? It was a good thing she now had Yanis, because if that was the case then she would need someone she trusted to step in and pick up the scalpel, if necessary.

'This is gorgeous. How's yours?'

'Wonderful. Would you like to try?'

He held out a forkful of beautifully pink rock salmon and she leaned forward to try it. It was quite an intimate moment, letting him feed her. Opening her mouth, gazing into his intense blue eyes as she took the food from his fork. She could feel her cheeks heating up and was grateful for the subtlety provided by the candlelight.

'Try some of mine.'

She tore off a small corner of her sourdough crust and loaded it with crab. Then she hand-fed Yanis, intensely aware of his lips enveloping her fingers.

Oh, my...

Her fingertips felt alive. Each nerve ending was tingling and fizzing with the need to be kissed by Yanis once again.

Her heart thudding in her chest and her mouth going dry, she suddenly wasn't sure if she'd be able to eat another bite! So she had a long drink of water and took a moment to just breathe and not meet Yanis's gaze.

I just need a second or two...

She kept her eyes on her plate, but all she could think about as she tried to calm her runaway heart was that night in Paris, stretched out naked beneath Yanis as his soft lips and gentle fingers explored her body. Arcing up towards him, her own hands hungry for the feel of him, needing him to fill her. Those lips...

'I...er... Excuse me. I just need the bathroom. Do you know where it is?' She stood up, her whole body thrumming with heat.

Yanis stood, too, placing his napkin down on the table. 'Are you all right?'

'Yes...yes. Just need to...erm... Where is it?'

Yanis pointed to a small dark door at the back of the restaurant that she could clearly see now had a silver *Ladies* sign on it.

'Thanks. Do carry on eating. I won't be long.'

And she hurried as quickly as she could to that door, opening it up, slipping inside and letting out a strangled breath or two as she gazed at her flushed reflection in the mirror above the sink. She turned on the cold tap and splashed water on her face, gazing at herself once again.

'What are you doing? Feeding Yanis? *Hand*-feeding him? Friendship, Samantha! *Friend. Ship.*'

Behind her, someone flushed the toilet and opened the cubicle door. A little old woman came out and smiled at her as she went to wash her hands.

'He's a lovely young man you're with this evening,' the woman said.

Sam recognised that she'd been seated at a table close to them. She nodded. 'Yes, he is.'

The old lady used the dryer to dry her hands and then, as she grasped the door handle to go out, turned once more to Sam and said, 'If I was fifty years younger I'd jump his bones so hard they'd shatter beneath me.'

She winked and left the room.

Sam stared after her, mouth agape, and then laughed.

Yanis felt guilty for not having told Sam the whole truth about what his family had said when they'd learned he was going to be a father. Of course there'd been surprise, exactly as he'd said, but then their voices and faces had filled with concern over the video link.

'Do you think the same thing could happen again?' his mother had asked.

He'd tried to remember that losing the babies with Giselle had not just happened to him and his wife, but to his family, too. They'd looked forward to becoming *grandmère* and *grandpère* or *oncle* and *tante*. They'd looked forward to seeing Yanis become a father and they'd all been brokenhearted by what had happened. Even more so when Yanis and Giselle had split up after so many years together.

They had loved Giselle. Adored her. Welcomed her into their homes. And now they had lost her, too, as Giselle couldn't bear to see them any more feeling as if she had let them all down. It wasn't true, of course, but grief and pain distorted things.

He'd wanted to tell Sam that his family would like to meet her, to put a face to her name, but he knew he wasn't ready. They were hardly in a relationship. He had no idea what this thing was that they had between them, and he didn't want to break the fragile nature of it.

Because he knew that it was breakable. Early days. Anything could go wrong.

And what if he introduced her to his family and they mentioned Giselle? Sam hadn't yet been told. She would feel she had been lied to. That he had deliberately kept important information from her. But how could he tell her about all that had gone wrong for him when she was already dealing with the possibility that their twins might develop TTTS, or that she might bleed out at any point if the placenta broke away from the lining of her womb?

So many things could go wrong. Not just physically, but mentally and emotionally. He knew he shouldn't allow his thoughts to linger on the doubts and fears, but it was something he associated with pregnancy now and it was a difficult habit to break.

As he waited for Sam to return from her bathroom break, he reminded himself that his relationship with Sam was different. Just because he'd lost his babies with Giselle, it did not mean the same would happen with Sam. There were issues, yes, but those could happen in any twin pregnancy. And there were plenty of identical twins out in the world. He needed to focus on positivity for the future, rather than the regret and pain from his past.

As Sam made her way back across the restaurant, he stood and pulled out her chair for her. 'Everything all right?'

She nodded. 'Everything's fine.'

CHAPTER FIVE

'LET'S MAKE A DIFFERENCE.'

Sam stood by the table in Theatre and made an incision in the leg to locate the femoral artery. Today she was hoping to use endovascular coiling to solve the problem of Maureen Bowman's posteriorcerebral aneurysm. It was an aneurysm that Maureen had lived with for some time, but as its size had remained static for many years, they had left it alone. In the last few weeks, however, the aneurysm had grown to just over seven millimetres and now was at greater risk of rupture.

'Guiding catheter, please.'

Her scrub nurse for the day, Sarah, passed it over and Sam gave a nod to the radiologist to move the fluoroscopic imager into position.

The adrenaline buzz she always got from surgery thrummed throughout her body. She was feeling good. Positive. And she knew it was down to the fact that nothing terrible had happened to her yet, and that she and Yanis were getting on quite well.

These last few weeks with Yanis had been enlightening. Yanis had been attentive and considerate, but not pushy with his opinions. Every day he saw her at work he checked to make sure she was feeling all right, and they'd spent a few hours in each other's company after work, too. Nothing heavy. Just walks in Richmond Park.

And once, he'd done her supermarket shop for her, because she'd been so tired. He'd come into her flat carrying all the bags and even unpacked everything for her. She'd been so grateful, and a little bit gobsmacked. Not used to anyone taking care of her like that.

Though she'd lived with her aunt for a while, after everything had come to light about her mother and her battle with Munchausen's by Proxy, she'd very much felt that her aunt was only doing her a favour. That she was tolerated. It had been almost as if her mother's sister had *blamed* Sam for what had happened to her mum. Having someone be kind was strange.

Once Yanis had dropped the shopping off, he'd asked her if she needed anything else before he left. Although she'd been absolutely desperate for someone to give her a shoulder massage, she'd simply shaken her head, said she was fine and then walked him to the door.

That had been awkward. Just like the night they'd gone out to that restaurant and he'd taken her home at the end of it. They'd had a really good chat. Got to know one another a bit more. And then there'd come the moment when she'd assumed most normal people would have kissed each other goodnight.

'Well, I've had a lovely evening, Yanis. Thank you,' she'd said. 'The food was delicious and the company was…enjoyable.'

He'd smiled at her, and in the evening darkness his eyes had twinkled. She'd almost felt that she should just kiss him and get it over and done with, but she'd known it wouldn't end there. She wanted him. Yearned for him. And if she'd leaned in for a kiss and pressed her lips to his she would have stopped thinking straight. She would have thrown caution to the wind and her clothes to her bedroom floor and they'd have been right back where they'd started.

So she'd let him lean in and drop a gentle kiss upon her cheek. She'd blushed and said goodnight, and with a great amount of self-control had closed the door, her heart pounding, her insides screaming at her that she could have had more than just delicious *food* this evening.

But maintaining his friendship and support through her pregnancy mattered more to her than anything else. At four months now, she was doing okay. Her belly was most definitely showing, and she'd had to tell her colleagues that she was expecting.

When they'd discovered that Yanis was the father, they'd all gaped, or gasped, and she'd received a range of comments. From *'You go, girl! Wow, lucky you!'* to a rather more amusing one from Judy, a junior doctor who was hoping to specialise in neurology, who had said, *'Well, of course you're expecting! I wouldn't get any sleep with him beside me either!'*

The support and care she was getting from her colleagues now was eye-opening. She'd spent so much of her life in a vacuum, feeling separated from everyone, feeling she could never connect with people, and yet here she was, and it seemed *everyone* was keeping an eye out for her.

It was nice. It was strange. And it made her see her relationship with Yanis with new eyes. No longer a secret. No longer a shameful hook-up she'd had in Paris. This relationship had become something more. Was it possible she could have a happy ending? Her work colleagues seemed to think that they made a good couple. Could it really be true?

She concentrated hard as she guided the catheter all the way up from the femoral artery to the posteriorcerebral artery, where the aneurysm was located.

'Micro-catheter, please.'

Slowly, and with great care, she inserted the smaller catheter directly into the aneurysm. Then the first coil went in, along the aneurysm's wall, to begin creating the frame. Once that was done, more coils were inserted, each progressively smaller, until she felt that she was done.

'Contrast dye.'

The radiologist inserted the dye to see if any flowed into the aneurysm, but there was no flow of dye to be seen, which was excellent.

'Okay, we're almost done.'

Sam withdrew the catheters and closed up. If all went as expected, Maureen would go home in a day or two and live the rest of her life as if this had never happened. It made Sam feel good to know that she had helped this poor woman. She'd been living with a time bomb, and Sam was having personal experience of how that felt right now.

Something could go wrong with her pregnancy at any minute. But so far she'd been okay, and she had an appointment this afternoon with her obstetrics consultant, Mr Meyer. Hopefully he would be able to reassure her.

She came out of surgery and went to get changed, and found Yanis just arriving for his shift.

'Hey,' she said.

'Good morning. *Ça va?*' He bent and laid a kiss upon her cheek in greeting, and once again she had to bite her bottom lip, to stop herself from reaching out and pulling him close.

'I'm good. You?'

'Very well. You're glowing.'

His eyes were bright and amused, and she liked it that she could make him look that way.

'Yes, well, aneurysm surgery first thing in the morning always gets my blood pumping.'

'No, it's more than that. How are the babies?' He laid his hand upon the swell of her abdomen and she had to fight not to lay her hand on his, too.

She met his gaze, smiled. 'They're good, as far as I know. They're telling me they want waffles with chocolate sauce.'

'Then you should give it to them.'

He turned away to open his locker, placing his rucksack inside and slipping off his jacket, revealing the almost skintight waistcoat he wore over his shirt beneath. He really did look yummy this morning. She found her gaze roving up and down his long body, remembering how it had felt that night in Paris.

What the hell is wrong with me? Hormones?

'I will.'

She opened up her own locker and grabbed her clothes from earlier, then went into a changing area to slip off her scrubs. She had rounds to do, to check on her post-operative patients from yesterday. Once dressed, she pulled her long red hair up into a twist and secured it with a clip.

When she came out of the cubicle, Yanis was waiting for her.

'I have some news,' he said.

'Oh?'

'I have rented a flat of my own.'

She raised her eyebrows. 'Whereabouts?'

'Near the park. It has two bedrooms. I'd like you to come and see it. I thought it was important that I put down some roots here.'

Seemed sensible…

'I'd like it if you could help me choose which room should become the nursery.'

She hadn't even thought about that. It was almost as if she had a mental block. But these babies might survive... She would actually have to think about where to put them after giving birth. Her own flat had two bedrooms, but the second one was loaded up with boxes and books. It would need a clear-out.

'Oh. Okay,' she said.

'Fancy coming round tonight?'

'You've moved in already?'

'I have.'

Going to Yanis's flat? Was that a risk? It was one thing to be at work together, and it was one thing to sit in a restaurant together—they were in public, after all—but in a private place... The last time they'd been in a private place together she'd got pregnant.

Well, I guess there's no risk of that happening again.

'What time?' she asked.

'I can pick you up at seven?'

'That's fine. Are you coming with me to see Mr Meyer today?'

'The appointment is at three?'

She nodded. If he didn't want to come, that would be fine. She'd do it on her own.

'I'll make sure I'm free, and if I get called into a surgery, I'll text you and let you know.'

* * *

He hadn't got called into a surgery. So here he sat with Sam and all the other expectant mothers at Mr Meyer's clinic.

Mr Meyer was apparently the go-to guy here at Barney's for multiple births. Sam knew he was good because she'd already re-searched him online. Just as she'd researched TTTS and placenta praevia and a whole host of other pregnancy complications that she didn't actually have.

It didn't hurt to be prepared.

Her mother had taught her that, at least.

When they got called through, they entered his room, shook his hand and sat down.

'So, you're expecting identical twins, it says here. Congratulations. How are you feeling, Mum?'

Sam blinked. It was the first time someone had called her *Mum* and it made her heart thud to realise that he was referencing *her*.

'Okay… No, I'm good. Hungry all the time.'

'Well, that's to be expected.' He smiled and tapped at his keyboard, bringing up the im-ages from her first ultrasound. 'The babies were both a good size…what, four weeks ago? They were each measuring the size of a singleton baby. I guess it would be a good thing to check on them again today, especially as they're sharing a placenta.'

She nodded.

'I'm sure you know the risks of that?' he said.

'We do,' she said.

'No prior pregnancies I should know about?'

Sam shook her head.

'Okay. I'll get that arranged in just a moment. Want to hop up onto the couch? I can check how you're measuring.'

Sam glanced at Yanis. He looked nervous. Anxious. Perhaps because it was here they would find out any bad news, whereas out in their real lives they could just pretend that everything was fine. Mr Meyer seemed to be the type of man who looked for issues so that he could treat them ahead of time.

She lay down on the couch and undid her trousers.

Mr Meyer had cold hands, which he apologised for, and then he palpated her abdomen slightly, smiling before reaching for a tape measure.

'Perfect. Exactly what I'd expect at this stage. Just lie there for a moment and I'll prep the ultrasound.'

He pulled the machine over and asked Yanis to kill the lights. The room went dark, except for the glow emanating from the screen.

Sam felt nervous. Sick. Just because she felt fine, it didn't mean that everything would be fine. It made her feel as if she was a little girl again. Lying there on a doctor's couch, waiting to be poked and prodded, oohed and aahed over…waiting to be told she would need surgery.

This is not the same. If I have surgery this time, it will be because I really need it.

Did that help her at all?

No.

She was so lost in her thoughts, Sam almost didn't feel the gel being applied, or the probe being placed on her stomach, until Mr Meyer turned the screen to show them the babies.

'Both looking very well. Again, both measuring as if they were singleton babies. Baby

A is ever so slightly bigger than Baby B, but only just. Nothing for us to worry about yet.'

'Good.'

The machine pumped out some more scan pictures. Mr Meyer passed a couple to Yanis. 'Any questions?'

'Is there anything Sam should be doing? Taking it easier? Maybe not doing long surgeries?'

Sam bristled inside. How *dared* he ask those questions? Hadn't Mr Meyer just said everything was fine?

Mr Meyer smiled at Sam. 'Whilst you're feeling good and the babies are happy you can carry on as usual—though obviously you'll need to take adequate rest breaks and make sure you stay hydrated and fed.'

She gave Yanis a look as if to say, *You see? You don't have to wrap me in cotton wool!*

'Do you have any questions, Sam?' Mr Meyer asked.

'How often will the babies be monitored from now on?'

'I'd like you to have a scan every two weeks. But if you have any concerns in between—if you don't feel them move, or something just doesn't feel right to you—you get in touch, okay?'

She nodded. She hadn't felt the babies move yet, but she'd read somewhere that mothers in their first pregnancies didn't normally feel movement until about eighteen or nineteen weeks. But the babies were measuring more than that. Why hadn't she felt them move? She knew nothing was wrong, because she'd just had the scan.

'How will I know that I feel them moving?'

Mr Meyer smiled. 'Oh, you'll know. It might feel like little fishes swimming at first, but eventually you'll feel kicks and the babies stretching. Pretty soon, too. Don't be surprised if you feel it by the end of the week. At the rate they're growing, it's pretty imminent, I'd say.'

Sam smiled. 'Okay.'

But she was nervous.

When Yanis arrived at her door that evening, she was still feeling pretty annoyed with him. 'Are you happy after trying to pull that stunt today?' she said, after she'd opened the door.

He frowned. 'I don't understand.'

'Trying to get my consultant to say I needed to slow down. You don't get to take charge of my life like that, do you understand? *I* decide how I work. *I* make the choices.'

He held up both his hands, as if surrendering. 'I'm sorry. I just wanted to make sure it was safe for the babies if you keep working at the rate you do.'

'I'm perfectly capable of making that decision myself.'

'I understand. And I'm sorry. But I'm allowed to worry. They're my babies, too.'

He gazed down at her growing abdomen with such a look of fear and concern that she felt awful for yelling at him. He was only trying to look out for them all.

'I know. Look, let's forget today. Why don't you just show me this flat of yours?'

'Deal.'

He drove her through Richmond and she allowed herself to enjoy the luxury of kicking back and having nothing to do. No patients. No surgeries. No stress. She could just enjoy the trees breaking into bloom, the signs of spring bursting forth in everyone's gardens. The shop windows with their Easter offers, and bunny rabbits and eggs and chicks in their displays.

This time next year I'll have two kids! If nothing goes wrong.

It still scared her. It seemed such an insurmountable task. How did parents do it? How would she mix motherhood and working? How would that work? Sure, they would get childcare, but what if she was in a very important surgery and she got a call from her child's nursery to say one of her children was sick with a fever? What if she got a call from their school to say she needed to come and pick them up that instant?

There were other surgeons who were parents. Perhaps she ought to ask them? They were best placed to give her answers. But would they think less of her for worrying about such a thing?

Who came first? The patient on the table? Or your child? Surely her own child should come first, but she couldn't possibly leave someone on the table. That was a life! It would mean playing tag with another neurosurgeon, but what if they weren't free either? And what if Yanis was in surgery, too?

'You're very quiet,' he said.

'Just thinking about things, that's all.'

'About the babies?'

She nodded.

'I think about them all the time, too.'

'You do? What sort of things do you think about?' She was intrigued.

'How we parent them. How we share them.'

She'd not thought too much about that. But he was right. How *would* they share them? Was she going to be a Monday-to-Friday mother and then Yanis got them weekends?

'Thanks,' she said.

'For what?'

'For giving me something else to worry about.'

He smiled and laid a hand upon hers. 'We will be okay.'

'Will we? Can you promise?'

He lifted her hand to his mouth and kissed the back of it. 'I can do my very best.'

Sam was very impressed with Yanis's flat. It was a decent size, with a large living area, a medium-sized kitchen, a bathroom that had both a shower and a bath, and the two bedrooms.

'Which do you think should be the nursery?' he asked. 'The room that faces the town, or the room that faces the park?'

It seemed a no-brainer to Sam. 'The room that faces the park, I guess. What do you think?'

He smiled. 'I agree.'

The room that faced the park had been painted by the previous tenant in a dark shade of green.

'It'll need a coat or two of paint. Brighten it up a little,' she said.

He nodded. 'Something neutral until we know what they are. Do you want to find out the sex of the babies?'

She'd not given that too much thought either. Her mind would briefly land on thoughts and ideas about the babies, but her unconscious was so busy telling her that everything could go wrong, and she could lose them at any point, that she'd spent a lot of time trying not to get attached to the idea of them actually existing.

Of course, she'd *wondered*. What it might be like to learn she was having two sons, or two daughters. Blue or pink?

But if she found out, if Mr Meyer told her what she was having, wouldn't that make them seem more real? Wouldn't that make her feel she was getting attached? If they found out what sex the babies were, then Yanis would want to start suggesting *names*, and that would make it really difficult. It would give them identities. Make them real people.

And if she lost them after they had names… that would hurt. It would hurt terribly even if they didn't have names. She couldn't imagine what it was like to lose a child. How did you get through something like that?

'I think I'd like it to be a surprise,' she said, thinking that was the diplomatic answer, rather than telling Yanis her fears.

'Oh. I'd hoped to find out.'

'You want to know?' she asked.

He nodded.

'Why?'

Yanis shrugged. 'I think it would make

them more real. More solid. We could decide on names.'

She smiled. 'Maybe they could tell you, but not me?'

'You think I could keep a secret like that?'

Sam laughed. 'Maybe not. You don't seem like the kind of man who keeps huge secrets. I think you're an open book.'

He gave a strange smile and walked over to the window that looked out over the park. 'Just think...one day we could be out there, walking with them through the trees. Playing with a kite or a football, or on bikes. Does that seem strange to you?'

It did. Sam hadn't had the kind of childhood that revolved around fun and normal childhood things. Her childhood had revolved around temperature spikes, sitting in doctors' offices, being made to eat and drink strange things that tasted funny, having blood drawn... There were fuzzy memories of a mask being held over her nose and mouth to send her off to sleep. Her friends had been nurses. Kindly ladies in colourful scrubs with teddy bear pins on their lapels.

How would she know what her child wanted?

'It does,' she said.

She rubbed at her abdomen, then stopped. What was that? That feeling? That weird sensation?

She must have frowned, because Yanis was instantly at her side.

'Sam, what's wrong?'

He was pulling his phone out of his pocket, ready to ring for God only knew what. An ambulance?

She grabbed his hand and laid it on her belly. 'Can you feel that? It's like little fishes. It's exactly what Mr Meyer said!'

A smile had formed upon her face without her realising. This was the joy of new life. The surprise of actually feeling these new lives *inside her.*

She'd spent years having doctors look for things to remove from her—tonsils, appendix, a rogue piece of cartilage that had actually been in her shoulder. There had been scans looking for tumours and growths, things that shouldn't have been there, things that were alien, and now she had this. Real life growing within her.

'I can't feel it…' Yanis sounded incredibly disappointed.

She tried to get him to press more firmly, but he couldn't feel what she could.

'Maybe the movements need to be stronger. Proper kicks before you'll be able to feel them.'

He nodded. 'But this is good. This is a good sign that they are strong. Healthy. Growing.'

'Yes.'

She looked up at him with tears in her eyes. She wasn't sure where the tears had come from. Were they tears of happiness for the babies? Or tears of happiness because after all these years of thinking she was broken and needed fixing, her body still knew how to do something right?

'I've changed my mind,' she said.

Yanis frowned. 'About the pregnancy?'

'No, about finding out what sex they are. I want to know, too.'

Suddenly it seemed vital.

His frown turned to a hopeful smile. 'You do?'

'Yes. I think I *need* to know now. I didn't before, but it's almost like…like they've persuaded me. Like they're saying, *Hi, we're here... You can't ignore us.*' She laughed. 'Does that make any sense at all?'

'*Oui, ma chérie.* It does.'

She felt the movements again, and laid a hand upon her abdomen. Yanis put his hand on her belly, too, and for a long time they just stood there, marvelling at the new lives they'd created, enjoying the knowledge that, for now, everything was perfectly all right. Nothing was going wrong. That there was hope of a bright and wonderful future.

Sam looked up at Yanis with joy and happiness in her eyes and saw the same emotions in him. *They* had done this. They had created these two new people together. She felt a connection with Yanis that she had never felt before. Something deep. Something meaningful. She knew that no matter how their future played out she would remember this moment for ever.

Yanis reached up and stroked the side of her face. His finger trailed down the side of her cheek and along her jaw.

She almost stopped breathing, staring up into his beautiful blue eyes and seeing his intent there and not wanting to stop it. Of course she had yearned for his touch—ever since he'd walked into her Theatre. But she had told herself he hadn't followed her here to pursue that, and then…then the pregnancy, the twins, the connection they had…

Why not do this?

As he moved closer, she lifted her hands to clasp him at the waist—a physical sign that he should proceed.

He lifted up her hair and his lips found her ear and the length of her neck, nibbling and kissing.

Her heart began to pound and she allowed herself to sink into the sensations he was creating, closing her eyes in ecstasy.

Oh, she needed this! All the stresses and strains of the last few weeks were melting away beneath the pleasure of his caress. It was as if all the tensions she'd been holding in were beginning to fade away into oblivion. Her skin felt electric, each nerve ending waiting for his caress, and when his lips found hers she moaned and threaded her fingers through his hair, holding on to him as if she never wanted to let him go.

He scooped her up and took her through to the main living area, where there were stacks of boxes, but also soft furnishings, and there he gently laid her down upon a pile of pillows, as if she was a precious jewel.

But Sam didn't want to be precious and she didn't want delicate. She'd waited for this for so long, denied herself the pleasure of him for too long, and so she reached for him and began to undo his shirt. She needed him. Needed to feel the heat of his skin, the hardness of his body. Needed to feel him against her. *In* her. If she filled herself with him...

I would feel complete.

She didn't stop to analyse that thought. It came and went in a single second, and she was too busy fiddling with buttons and his belt.

'Slow down, Sam. There's no rush,' he whispered as he stared into her eyes. 'This is not like before. You have no plane to catch. No need to run. We have all the time in the world.'

She smiled and let out a sigh.

She was used to making this a hurried thing. Something she did with a stranger to answer a need, making sure to leave before questions could be asked, before commitment could be implied. She'd always just satisfied her need in the moment. It had never been part of something more.

But whether she chose to like it or not, what she had with Yanis was something much deeper. It had a commitment to it. This wasn't going to be some flash in the pan. This wasn't going to be some quick hookup and she'd never see him again. He was in her life permanently now. He had seeded two babies into her womb and she worked with him. They shared patients and a place to be. He understood her world and her passion and her needs.

He was right.

What would it feel like if she took this slowly? It had been mind-blowing the last time, because they'd both been feeling hurt and lost and had sought comfort in each other. This time it was going to be different.

'Okay.'

She smiled and rolled him over onto his back, so that she sat on top of him. His hands held her hips as she slowly began to undo the buttons of her blouse. She liked him watching her. Liked seeing the pupils of his eyes dilate as she revealed more and more of herself.

'Tu es si belle.'

'What does that mean?'

'It means you're so beautiful.'

She blushed and reached around her back to undo her bra.

'Non,' he said. 'Let me.'

And he sat up and stared hungrily into her eyes as he reached around and expertly undid the clasp.

'You've done that before,' she said.

He smiled at her. 'Not my first time.'

She laughed and tossed back her hair as his hands moved to her back, supporting her as his lips trailed across her chest and his fingertips tickled her sides before coming forward to her breasts. The heat of his breath and the scrape of his teeth against her skin was exquisite, and when he lay back she went with him and pressed her mouth to his, her tongue exploring the depths of him, dancing in a tango with his.

This was all such a delicious delight but she

needed more. Wanted more. She was hungry for a man in a way she had never been before.

Yanis gently turned her onto her back and his expert fingers made swift work of the zip of her skirt, pulling it down to reveal her lacy underwear. His lips kissed her belly button, the swell of her abdomen, and his fingertips gently traced the curve of it, this fascinating development of new life that he had helped create.

And then his lips went lower.

It was exquisite agony through the lace. She wanted direct contact. To feel his tongue upon her swollen, hungry flesh. But he teased her mercilessly, until she began to beg him.

'Yanis…*please*!' She'd never begged for anything in her entire life, but she was begging now and she didn't care.

Slowly, with a wicked smile, he began to peel down her underwear, removing them from her legs and tossing them to one side. And then, just when she thought that, *yes*, she would get everything of him that she wanted, the pleasure that she sought, he stood up.

She almost thought he was going to leave

her in that state, which was cruel. 'What are you doing?' she asked.

'Taking off my clothes.'

'Oh...' She smiled, lying there naked and wanton. 'Want some help?'

He held out a hand and she clasped it, and then he pulled her upwards into a standing position. She kissed him, mouth to mouth, her fingers unfastening his belt, finding the button of his trousers, the zip, feeling the hard swell of him beneath the fabric and wanting the gift inside. She reached into his trousers and caressed him, making him gasp at her touch, and then she was kneeling in front of him, pulling down his trousers, helping him step out of them and stroking his erection through the fabric of his boxers.

She would tease him the way he'd teased her. It seemed only fair.

She brushed her lips over the taut fabric and looked up at him. Yanis was breathing hard. He was magnificent. All of him. Clothed and unclothed.

Was this really happening? For most of her life, all Sam had thought was that people only needed her medically. That her only use was to be picked over for information, or to use her professional skills to heal someone. On a personal level, she had always kept herself and her heart and soul remote from others. It had just seemed easier. Safer.

And now she found herself in strange territory. Dipping her toe into unknown waters. But she felt *good* about it—and that was the oddest and most surprising thing. Was that because *she* had changed? Or was it because this was Yanis, and with him she felt that it was safe to do so?

Either way, right now it didn't matter...

Afterwards she lay in his arms as he lazily stroked the skin over her hips.

'Sam?'

'Yes?'

'I notice you have laparotomy scars.'

She tensed, swallowing. 'Yeah.'

'What were they for?'

She shrugged. 'Something I had done as a child. Exploratory stuff. They weren't sure what was going on.'

She'd known, though. Sam had known well enough what was going on. There had been nothing physically wrong with her except for what her mother was doing. Starving her so that she would have *'unexplained weight loss'*. Making her drink weird concoctions to give her *'unexplained stomach pains'*. All so that her mother could act the angst-ridden parent who was just so terribly grateful to all the doctors for looking after her and comforting her while Sam was in surgery.

The laparotomy had been the final straw for Sam. She'd had enough. She'd finally spoken out. After the doctors had gathered around her bed to tell Sam and her mother that they'd found nothing conclusive and her mother had gone home—no doubt to plan her next medical move—Sam had asked to speak to one of the doctors and told him everything, fearing that he wouldn't believe her. Only he had. He had listened. And when her mother had turned up for her next visit, the police had been waiting.

But to tell Yanis that…? Even though they'd just shared something so intimate she should be able to tell him anything…? It wasn't just about entrusting him with that information, it was whether she would be able to cope with

the horror and pity she would see in his eyes.
That she would never be able to stand.

'And the appendectomy?'

'Same. Done as a child.'

'You spent a lot of time in hospitals when
you were younger, then?'

'You could say that.'

'Is that where you found your passion for
medicine?'

She thought for a moment. 'It made me
want to understand the human body. What
it was capable of. What it could create. What
diseases it could fight. Its strengths, its weak-
nesses.'

'You are strong—you know that, right?'

'Am I?'

'Of course. Two new lives you carry within
you. That's a marvellous and wondrous thing.'

'It's a scary thing. I have a whole new respect for mothers.'

'You didn't have respect for mothers before?'

'Yes. I just never really *knew*, if that makes
any sense?'

'What about your own mother?'

'We don't really talk.'

'Why not?'

'It's a long story. If you don't mind, I'd really rather not sully this perfect moment by speaking about her right now.'

Yanis had nuzzled into her neck. 'Okay.'

Lying there, sated, was everything she needed in that moment.

CHAPTER SIX

'YOU'VE GOT A SURGERY?'

Yanis was scrubbing in for a surgery on a private patient when Sam found him.

'I have.'

'On who?'

'A private patient.'

'Oh, right. Anything interesting?'

'Craniometaphyseal dysplasia.'

It was a rare condition that presented as a thickening or overgrowth of bones in the skull. It was something that would continue throughout life.

'Is it her first surgery?' Sam peered through the viewing pane at the patient, already laid out on the table.

'No, it's her fourth.'

'Poor kid. Need an assist?'

'I'm good. I've got a resident and a student in with me, so it might be crowded.'

'Okay. It's my twenty-week scan later, at two p.m. Are you going to be free for that?'

Yanis glanced at the clock, clearly doing some mental maths. 'I should be.'

'I don't want to go in on my own.'

He glanced at her, hearing the fear in her voice. She looked well. Even though she was only technically five months pregnant now, she actually looked more like six or seven. If there was an issue, surely she would have said?

'Is there a problem?' He hoped not. Not now that they were so close! If they could just get to twenty-four weeks, then they'd stand a good chance.

'No, I just don't want to go in by myself in case there's bad news.'

'Why would there be bad news?'

'Things like that just happen to me.'

And to me.

But he had to be strong for both of them. Be there as he had tried to be before. Remain positive.

'You'll be fine. The babies will be fine. I promise.'

He knew it wasn't a promise he should

make. He didn't know they would be fine. How could he? No one would know until the scan. And this time, hopefully, they would find out the sex, too. At the last scan, a couple of weeks ago, the twins had been positioned in such a way it had been impossible to be sure. The sonographer had said she could make a guess, but neither of them wanted to rely on guesses. Certainty was what both of them needed.

'I'll be there, *ma chérie.*'

She nodded. 'Good luck with your surgery.'

He smiled. *'Merci.'*

When she'd left, the smile dropped from his face as he concentrated on scrubbing properly, but his thoughts worried away at him. He was dreading this scan. He dreaded all of them. Each time they went, he tried to remain focused and positive for Sam, but inside he was being torn apart.

What if this was the scan that showed a problem? What if this was the scan where they saw they'd lost one or both of the babies? What if this was the scan when he would have to come clean with Sam and tell her everything? He couldn't imagine upsetting her like that, scaring her like that, but didn't she deserve the truth?

He wanted to tell her *so badly*! But each time he thought about discussing with her what had happened, he saw her own doubts, her own fears, her own certainty that something terrible was going to happen, and he didn't want her thinking that way. He'd seen it tear Giselle apart and he couldn't watch it tear Sam apart!

He'd not been able to save his relationship with his wife after that, and right now he and Sam were doing well. He was beginning to have some hope of happiness again. If he told her everything, would he ruin it all? He didn't want to ruin anything. Being with Sam was... almost indescribable. She was such a strong woman. He could see it, even if she didn't. He admired her. Not just as a surgeon, but for her bravery in the face of uncertainty. An uncertainty that hung over him every day like a dark cloud.

The pressure was immense. To be the one with broad shoulders so others could lean on you. Being the one to provide one of those shoulders to cry on, or a soft place to fall, a safe place in which they could vent their fears and worries.

It was a load he was happy to carry, but sometimes—just sometimes—he wondered if there was a place *he* could go to vent? He wanted it to be Sam, but she needed him to be strong right now, so he kept all of his fears and worries tightly bound up inside.

Yanis moved into Theatre and checked with Aarav, the anaesthetist, that the patient was good to go.

Aarav nodded. 'Ready to rock and roll.'

'Okay, let's do it.'

The babies were kicking and she was finding it hard to concentrate. Sam rubbed at her abdomen, pushing down on what felt like a foot and smiling as she reviewed a patient's notes.

'So, your GP has referred you to me because you're having some dizzy spells, is that right?'

Molly Jacobs was a woman in her early forties. Slight, pale and fidgety. 'Yes, that's right. They just come out of nowhere.'

'And how long does each of these dizzy spells last?'

'Not long. Minutes...or just seconds. But the after-effects last a week or two. It takes me ages to be able to stand up, and when I do, I have to lean on things, because the world seems tipped on its axis. It's like being drunk, when I've not had the joy of a night out.'

Sam smiled. 'And how long have you been having these episodes?'

'Three to four months. They're debilitating. I've had so much time off work.'

'What do you do?'

'I'm a preschool teacher.'

'And it says here your GP first suggested it was labyrinthitis?'

'Yes.'

'Any hearing loss?'

'I don't think so, but I've developed tinnitus. I can hear sounds inside myself.'

'Any headaches? Blurred vision?'

'Headaches for sure. And my eyes get tired.'

'Hmm... Okay. Well, I'm going to send you

for an MRI, just to make sure you haven't got anything going on that shouldn't be.'

'Like what?'

'It could be all manner of things. It could be something as simple as Ménière's disease, which affects the balance, but with symptoms like these, we like to perform a scan just to rule out other conditions.'

'Such as?'

Sam smiled. 'Let's not worry about what it might be until we know what it's not. Deal?'

Molly nodded. 'When do I get the MRI?'

'Today. You're already booked in.' She handed over a slip of paper. 'Take that to Reception and the lady there will direct you. You can go home afterwards, and if everything's fine, your GP will let you know. But if we find anything, then I'll get in touch to arrange further treatment, okay?'

'All right. Thank you, Ms Gordon.'

'No problem. Best of luck.'

Molly left and Sam stood to stretch and gaze out of the hospital window. From her office, she could see down into the atrium, and across from there to the older rehabilitation buildings, where her friend Gil worked. She hadn't seen him for a while and hoped he was okay. Normally they met up once a week, just to check in, but what with her pregnancy and spending time getting to know Yanis, that had fallen a little to the wayside.

Feeling guilty, she sat down again and picked up the phone, dialling the extension for Gil's office.

He picked up almost immediately.

'Hey, Gil, it's Sam.'

'Hey! How's tricks?'

'Good. Haven't seen you for a while… Just wanted to check in and make sure you're okay?'

'Busy, as always. How about you? Everything going all right?'

'Yes. Got my anomaly scan this afternoon.'

He must have heard the tension and the worry in her voice, because he said, 'You'll be just fine. The babies have been doing okay so far. How's Yanis holding up?'

'He's good.'

'I like him. I've met him a couple of times when he's come over to the unit to follow up on a patient.'

'He gets your approval, huh?'

'He does. He really cares for you, you know?'

'What makes you say that?'

'The way he speaks about you. It's this look he gets in his eyes… I don't know. Don't ask me to name it. I'm no expert in the human heart.'

The way Gil's Australian accent drew out the word *heart* cheered her soul.

'You almost sound poetic.'

Gil laughed. 'It's the new me.'

'We should meet up for lunch one day. In the atrium.'

'We should. I'll call you another time. Right now, I've got a patient waiting. You'll call me and let me know how the scan goes, right?'

'Sure thing.'

'Bye.' And he put down the phone.

She felt better for having checked in with him. She had done her duty as his friend and colleague. She didn't have many close friends, and he was the only one who truly knew what had happened to her.

Sam knew she would have to tell Yanis

at some point—but when? After the babies had been born? Before? She wasn't sure. It was such a huge thing to share. So deeply personal. And right now they were creating something new. Not just new life, but a relationship of sorts, and she kind of wanted to see where that was going. She would have to trust him one hundred per cent before she could tell him everything.

Sam picked up the phone and called through to the receptionist. 'Can you send my next patient in, please?'

The patient came in alone. Perry Lombard. A forty-eight-year-old man who had been referred to her by his GP for trigeminal neuralgia. TN was characterised by sudden, severe and extremely sharp lasting pains in the side of the face. The attacks could be so debilitating and so awful that patients reported that they were unable to do anything until they had passed.

'Hello, Mr Lombard, I'm Samantha Gordon. How are you today?'

'All right for the moment.'

'I see you're here because of your trigeminal neuralgia. Why don't you tell me about how it's been affecting you?'

'I've had it for over a year. It came on suddenly. We couldn't work out what had triggered it. Now I get multiple attacks every week.'

'How many attacks a week, would you say?'

'Sometimes every day. Sometimes every other day. It depends… But it's really beginning to affect my mental health now, and I don't think I can keep going on if the rest of my life is going to be like this.'

That, unfortunately, was something she heard a lot regarding this particular condition, when it affected someone so brutally.

'Your doctor gave you carbamazepine? How did that work out?'

Mr Lombard sighed. 'Initially it seemed to work. It didn't get rid of all the pain, but it lessened it for a while. Still enough to damn well hurt, but I could do things. I could go out with my wife. I could work in the garden. I could stay upright, for God's sake. But after a month or two of taking it I began to suffer side effects.'

'What kind?'

'Dizziness. I felt like I couldn't think straight. Like my head was all woolly. And it made me feel sick to my stomach, I could barely eat, and I've lost weight because of it.'

'It says here in your GP's letter that he then tried you on gabapentin. Was that any better for you?'

'It helped me eat. But it gave me problems in other areas.'

'Such as what?'

Mr Lombard looked uncomfortable. 'Sexually.'

Sam nodded. That sometimes happened. The ability to reach orgasm could be a struggle. 'And what do you hope to gain from today?'

He shrugged. 'I don't know. Some ideas, I guess, on what I can do next. Medication seems to just add problems, and the neuralgia is problem enough! I guess I asked to be referred to you to see if there were any other options. Surgical, or not.'

'There are a few things we can try if medications aren't working. There are percutaneous procedures that can offer some relief. There's radiosurgery and decompression procedures we could try, all done under a general anaesthetic.'

'What's the easiest one?'

She smiled. 'Well, of the percutaneous procedures, we could try a glycerol injection.'

Sam brought up an image on her computer screen that showed a cut-through slide of the human head, highlighting the branches of the trigeminal nerve.

'This here is called the Gasserian ganglion—it's where the three main branches of the trigeminal nerve join together. We inject glycerol directly into it, in the hope that it will disrupt the pain signals that travel along it.'

He nodded. 'How long would I be in hospital for?'

'Just the day. You could be home in the evening.'

'What other options are there?'

'There's a procedure called radiofrequency

lesioning, where we use a needle to apply heat directly to that ganglion, or we could use balloon compression. We pass a tiny balloon along a thin tube through the cheek. Then we inflate it around the ganglion and squeeze it.'

'So, basically, you think it's this ganglion thing that's causing all my issues?'

'Applying treatment to that area seems to have good outcomes.'

'Is it dangerous?'

'All surgeries have an element of risk, of course, but these are the more basic procedures we'd carry out before we'd consider anything else.'

'And if they worked, would that be for ever?'

'That can depend on each case. For some people the pain relief lasts for years, for others it's months or weeks, and in some cases there's no relief at all.'

Mr Lombard sighed. 'It's a lot to take in, isn't it?'

'It is.'

'Would I be a candidate for these procedures?'

'I would be happy to put you forward for treatment. Clearly you've tried medication, and that's not working for you, and if the condition is beginning to affect your mental health then it's time to do something.'

'But if these procedures don't work, we could still try something more radical?'

She nodded.

'Okay. Well, I'd like to think it over. Talk about it with the wife, you know?'

Sam understood. 'Of course. Here's a print-out of all those procedures I've mentioned. Take it home, discuss it, and then contact my secretary on the number at the bottom to let me know what you decide. There's no rush. All right?'

She stood up and reached over to shake his hand.

Mr Lombard smiled at her. 'You've been a great help—thank you very much.' He looked down at her belly. 'Will you be around to do my surgery?'

She laughed. 'I've still got a few months to go, so yes, I will.'

'All right. Well, it was nice to meet you, Ms Gordon.'

'You too, Mr Lombard.'

She watched him go and rubbed at her abdomen. The babies were kicking a lot today. She liked that. It reassured her in ways she hadn't expected. She was getting used to the idea that she was going to become a mother now. It had been so scary at first, and knowing that she had Yanis supporting her had become important. It was good to have someone in her corner. Someone who truly meant it. Who genuinely cared for her.

She saw it in her patients. If they had support, had someone sitting by their bedside, rooting for them to get well, it impacted on their healing time. Those who had a good support network healed faster and better, with fewer residual side effects, than those who had no one.

She'd thought at the start of this that she'd have no one.

But she was beginning to see that that wasn't true at all.

His dysplasia case had overrun, but finally he was out of Theatre. Yanis scrubbed and dried off his hands, then checked the time. Fifteen minutes late for the anomaly scan.

His phone showed four text messages from Sam and two missed calls.

Cursing under his breath, he rushed to the lifts that would take him down to the floor he needed and punched the button. The lifts seemed to be taking an age, so he headed for the stairwell and ran down the stairs instead, bursting into the waiting room for the antenatal clinic all out of breath and causing everyone to turn and look at him.

He scanned the faces and saw Sam over in the far corner. Her frown disappeared and a relieved smile crossed her face.

'I'm so sorry I'm late!' He dropped a kiss on her cheek and sat down next to her. 'Have I missed it?'

'No. Thankfully, they're overrunning, too. What took you so long? I thought I was going to have to go in on my own.'

Whispering to her, to avoid being overheard, he said, 'The dysplasia case had a few complications. Her BP dropped multiple times and we were having problems with anaesthesia.'

'What kind of problems?'

'It seemed way too light. She needed more and more. I was beginning to think we would have to stop the surgery to give her body chance to recover.'

'Did you finish?'

'*Oui.* Thank goodness. How are you doing? How are my babies doing?' He laid a hand on her belly and smiled at a well-timed kick right in the centre of his palm.

'We're all fine. Let's hope they tell us the same when we go in.'

'I'm sure they will.'

He pressed his lips into her hair and breathed her in, trying to savour this moment. Everything was fine right now, and it felt good to just revel in it with her.

The closeness they'd been creating between them was to be cherished, knowing that she felt something for him, too. Ever since they'd had sex in his flat, their relationship had gone in a different direction from just colleagues and friends to something more...

intimate. He liked it. Liked her. Liked the way she made him feel. Liked sneaking glances at her. Watching her smile, or flip her hair, or laugh.

Sam could be very intense at work. Dedicated. Driven. It was nice to see her take her foot off the pedal occasionally and relax and be herself.

'Samantha Gordon?'

They both stood up, and once again Yanis felt his stomach twist in a familiar fear. He'd been to every scan so far with Sam, and they both kept an eye on the blood flow and amniotic fluid around the twins, and each time he knew they could go in and hear something devastating.

He'd spent far too much time at home researching TTTS and he knew the awful risks—had read some terribly upsetting blogs from parents who had been in the same situation as them. Parents who had lost one or both of their babies.

He had felt their pain and wept, and he couldn't believe he was walking that same tightrope once again.

He told himself that he had to draw strength

from Sam. From how she was acting. How she was telling him how she felt. How much the babies were moving. All of these were positives.

Sam lay down on the couch and bared her growing abdomen. She was a good size now, and looked healthy.

The sonographer began moving the probe over her abdomen.

'How does it look?' asked Yanis. He could see two heartbeats, so that was good. That made him relax somewhat.

'Twin A is measuring at just under twenty-seven centimetres and is about thirteen ounces, and Twin B is measuring at about twenty-four centimetres and eleven ounces.'

'That's good, right?'

'They're doing well. But there's less fluid around twin two, so we'll want to keep a closer eye on that. Up till now they've both been measuring about the same, according to your records, and now we're beginning to see a difference.'

'Is it TTTS?' asked Sam.

'You'll have to speak to your consultant.

He'll probably want you scanned weekly, instead of fortnightly.'

'Oh...'

'But the babies are healthy for now?' asked Sam.

'Their heartbeats are strong. You've noticed plenty of movement?'

Sam nodded. 'Yes.'

'That's good. Do you want to know the sex?'

Yanis squeezed Sam's hand. 'We do.'

'You're expecting identical girls.'

'Girls?' Sam let out a breath.

Daughters.

He was going to have two daughters.

Something welled up deep inside him and his desire to protect them all intensified. He lifted Sam's hand to his mouth and kissed it, fighting back the tears that threatened to show. Now the babies were even more real, and they needed their *papa* to be strong for them.

'I'll send copies of the scan and my report straight up to Mr Meyer,' said the sonographer.

'Thank you.'

Everything else checked out. Their brains, their bladders, their lungs, the length of their femurs... All the things that were checked showed that the babies were doing okay. The placenta was still low, though...

Sam and Yanis walked out of the scan room on a muted high. Elation at finding out they were expecting girls, but also caution because of the difference in size and the suggestion that now they'd be on weekly scans instead of fortnightly.

'It could get worse, Yanis.'

'But it might not be. Twin A might have just had a growth spurt and her sister will have caught up the next time you're checked.'

She nodded, but her face showed that she wasn't sure. 'Her sister... I can't believe it's going to be girls.'

'I know. We'll have to think of some names.'

Sam shook her head. 'No, we can't. Not yet. It'll be too awful if we name them and...' Her voice trailed off. 'And the worst happens.'

He sucked in a breath and then let it out slowly. He'd been through the worst happening. They'd named Jacques before they'd lost him. Had that made it worse? Surely losing a child at this stage would be terrible even if they didn't have a name?

Could this happen to him again? Was it always going to happen to him? The idea of watching it happen again was just too awful to contemplate. Her reminder that it could all still go wrong was just too much.

'I'm sorry. I have to go check on my patient.'

Sam watched him go, feeling suddenly hurt. Had she upset him by suggesting that they might still lose these babies? She was only being practical. He needed to know the risks. He needed to know that not everything was straightforward when it came to her body, though thankfully her womb was one of the areas her mother hadn't deliberately set out to injure, and Sam had been living with her aunt by the time her periods began.

Perhaps he was fed up with her worrying constantly and wondering why she couldn't just be happy and embrace the joy of carrying their children.

She wanted to. She wanted to be like a

normal pregnant mother-to-be. She wanted to delight in her blooming belly, in every kick. She wanted to decorate nurseries and spend ages flicking through baby name books, looking for the perfect name. Only she couldn't. She'd been on fortnightly scans and now it would be weekly.

Every other mother only got two scans. Two! One just after the first trimester and a second one at around twenty-one weeks. But, oh, no, not Sam. She had 'issues'.

Twins could develop life-threatening TTTS, where the donor baby became small and weak and the recipient twin became huge and suffered heart problems, or even worse. She also had a low-lying placenta that looked as if it wasn't going to move, and that meant she could begin to bleed out at any time, so they had to keep an eye on that, too.

If the likelihood of TTTS increased, she might have to have laser ablation, to try to sort out the blood flow for the twins, and that procedure carried risks, too. The twins could die. It might not work, or only work for a short time, and she was only twenty-one weeks pregnant. Nowhere near the safety line after which her babies might try to survive if they had to be delivered early.

The idea that she might only be mere weeks away from delivery startled her and made her feel sick....

She wasn't ready. Nothing was ready. Yanis had bought a few things and she'd told him off for doing that. But otherwise they had nothing. No cribs, no car seats, no nappies, no bottles, no clothes. Should she start preparing? Preparing for them to live?

Sam headed up to the neurosurgery floor and went straight to the doctors' station. She booted up the internet and in a fit of optimism started buying baby things. Basic things. A place for them to sleep. Some clothes for newborns, some nappies, a double buggy, two cots... She arranged for them to be sent to her home. Once it was done, she felt marginally better. It might show Yanis that she was looking ahead. That she was hoping for a good outcome, no matter how much she worried out loud.

But she couldn't silence the small voice in the back of her head that told her she'd somehow tempted fate.

* * *

The post-operative ward was usually a nice, quiet and peaceful place where patients recovered from surgery. Having already spent some time in the ICU, the post-operative ward was a positive step forward for them. It meant that they were out of the danger zone of that crucial first twenty-four hours post-op and could start thinking about either going home or heading to the neurological rehabilitation suite.

Sam waited for Yanis to be free after talking to his patient. 'Could I have a quick word?' she asked.

'Of course.'

He followed her over to the nurses' station, a look of enquiry on his face.

'I wanted to apologise,' she began.

He frowned. 'For what?'

'For being me. For always thinking the worst is going to happen. I get that you're not like that. I get that you're the optimist here. It's just that I'm used to thinking the worst, especially when it comes to my health, and...' she paused for a moment, debating

'... I'd like the opportunity to tell you why I'm like that.'

'Okay...'

Sam looked around them. 'Not here, though. My place? Tonight? I could cook. Pasta or something.'

Her heart was racing at the thought of what she was going to do, but she knew she would have to do it. Yanis was going to find out sooner or later. He had to know. These were his children she was carrying—he had a right to know just who he'd got involved with. This wasn't just about her any more, and now that everything was getting scarier she felt that if anything were to go horribly wrong and he found out *afterwards*, she wouldn't be able to live with the guilt. Knowing that she should have been upfront with him from the very beginning.

'I'll be there,' he said.

She nodded. 'Great. That's great. Thank you.'

He reached out, took her hand. 'You do know you don't have to apologise to me, don't you?'

'Don't I?'

'*Non.* Your worrying…it just goes to show how much you care. It shows how much you love the twins already, so why would I complain about that?'

She shrugged, not knowing what to say. He was being so nice to her. So kind. But then, he always had been, ever since they'd met. Maybe she had to accept that that was just how Yanis was? That she had to let him be that way with her, and that maybe not everyone she allowed to get close was out to hurt her?

When the doorbell rang, she still wasn't sure she was ready to do it. But when he came in and kissed her on the cheek, and presented her with a bottle of non-alcoholic wine and a small bouquet of flowers, she knew that she must.

Yanis had to understand where she was coming from. He had to know who she was. He was possibly about to become a father and co-parent with her, and that sort of relationship didn't deserve secrets.

She served up the food—a basic pasta dish, made with a jar of sauce and some Parmesan cheese grated on top—and poured the non-alcoholic wine into their glasses.

'Cheers.' She held hers up. 'To healthy babies.'

'To healthy babies.' He clinked her glass with his, smiled and took a sip.

The wine did nothing to make her feel more confident, of course, but it did help settle her churning stomach, which was making it difficult for her to eat.

'I need to tell you something, Yanis. Something about me and my past and how it's made me the person that I am today.'

'All right.'

'I'm telling you because I think I can trust you—and, well, because we're having babies together, hopefully, and I'd like to think that you will always be in my corner.'

'Of course I will. What is it, Sam?'

She took in a deep breath and laid down her fork. 'You remember I told you about when I was a child? About how I spent a lot of time being ill?'

He leaned forward, resting his elbows on the table, his eyes intense as he listened to her. *'Oui.'*

'Well, the bit I left out was the fact that I wasn't really ill. At least not really.'

He frowned. He didn't understand.

She knew she had to plough on. Get it out. Tell him everything.

'My mother made me sick,' she whispered. Saying the words out loud somehow cemented the truth of it once again, and the shame she felt almost swallowed her whole. 'My mother suffered from Munchausen's by Proxy.'

Yanis closed his eyes in dismay, then reached out and held her hand, clasping it in his strong, firm fingers. 'What did she do to you?'

'You've seen my scars. She convinced doctors to do several exploratory laparoscopies, and I had my appendix removed, my tonsils removed. I had endoscopies, blood tests, stool tests, urine tests... I was poked, prodded, scanned. She used to give me salt water to make me sick, so she could take me to the doctor. She would sometimes starve me, only feeding me small amounts of soup, so that I would suddenly lose weight.'

Yanis shook his head in silence.

'I think it started when my father left. When my mum discovered she was pregnant he didn't stick around, and she was bereft. She had a difficult pregnancy with me, and kept going into premature labour, so they kept her in hospital on bed rest. It started there, her therapist told me. With the attention she got from the doctors and nurses. She had no one else, so the caring they showed her in making sure that I was all right seemed to get confused in her head. She believed that their caring natures actually showed her the love she craved. When I was born and she was sent home, things were all right for a while. She would take me for walks and complete strangers would stop her and coo over me, ask her how she was doing and if I slept through the night. She flourished under their praise. But then I got older, and the attention disappeared. She craved it. And that's when she started doing things to me.'

'Oh, Sam...'

She smiled and squeezed his hand tight, glad of his reassurance. Glad that he hadn't withdrawn, appalled.

'The doctors would see her sitting by my hospital bed and think that she was the most attentive mother, constantly talking to me, trying to keep me cheerful, but she wasn't doing that. She was just whispering instructions. *"Lie still. Don't move. Try not to eat the food. Don't speak. Don't answer their questions."'*

Sam shook her head.

'When I was in hospital for that last laparoscopy, she was already planning my next "illness". She was trying to convince the doctors I had a brain tumour. She told them I was having seizures, that I'd said my vision was blurry, that I had headaches. I was even already booked in for an MRI. But after that laparoscopy I was scared, and I told the doctors everything. They waited for her to come in on her next visit and had the police and social services waiting. When I recovered, they took me away from her and placed me with my aunt.'

'Thank God that they did. And you were all right?'

'Apart from the scars she'd left me with. Apart from the fact that for years I'd been brainwashed to think that I was faulty. That I was broken. That I needed fixing. I had a lot of therapy afterwards, and I struggled to trust people because of what she did.'

'I'm glad you've trusted me enough to tell me.'

'You needed to know. I'm pregnant. We're having two babies and you need to know why I always think the worst. Why I always suspect that something is going to go wrong. It's my defence mechanism, if that makes any sense. If I assume things are going to go badly, then when it happens it hurts less.'

'Does that really work?' he asked, sounding really interested in the possibility.

She shrugged. 'I tell myself it does. I thought I'd escaped before things got too bad, but still I find myself in this situation: pregnant with problems. My mother had a difficult pregnancy and nearly lost me—what if the same happens to me?'

'How do you know your mother didn't cause the pregnancy problems herself?'

She shook her head. 'I don't know.'

'From what you've told me, it's possible

that she did. Your mother's pregnancy should have no bearing on your own.'

'But it doesn't stop me from worrying, Yanis. What if I'm like her?'

'That's impossible.'

'How do you know that?'

'Because you're a healer. A doctor. You make people better... You've never caused anyone harm. Do you attention-seek? *Non.* You're not like her and never will be.'

'But I worry in case I'm broken for real. What if I'm not meant to have children? What if my womb is so terribly faulty that it won't get to the end of these nine months? What if my mother was right all along?'

Yanis got up from the table and came around it to her side. Kneeling down in front of her, he laid his hands on her swollen belly, kissed it. 'You're scared. I get that. I am, too. But the Samantha Gordon I know is *nothing* like the woman you've just described. You're strong. Beautiful in heart. Your love and concern for these babies shine through. You could never harm them. I believe that more than I believe anything.'

She smiled. 'Thank you.'

'Thank you for telling me. For trusting me enough to tell me. That's a big step, Sam. A *big* step.'

She nodded. Hoping that he wouldn't prove her wrong.

CHAPTER SEVEN

'WHERE ARE WE GOING?' Sam asked, when Yanis turned up at her home, told her to put on her jacket and get ready for a walk.

'Richmond Park.'

'Why?'

'To remind you that there is happiness and life to be found *outside* of the hospital.'

'Oh.' She smiled, then laughed, and grabbed at the lightweight jacket that was hanging over the balustrade.

Yanis drove them through the busy streets, away from the centre of town and out towards the park, finding a nice parking spot down a small road. As she waited for him to lock up the car, he went to the boot, opened it and pulled out a picnic basket.

'We're having a picnic?' she asked.

'We are.'

'Okay...'

It was entertaining for him to watch the

strains of the day slowly ease away from Sam's face as they walked through the park. Yanis reached for her hand and clasped it in his, and with the early summer sun beating down upon their faces, he felt the cares of the world begin to dissipate. This was nice. This time away from the hospital.

It would be all too easy for them to allow their entire lives to revolve around work and patients. Their jobs were intense. Too intense. It was extremely important that they had downtime. Time to relax. To shake off their worries and their cares and just enjoy being in each other's company.

'Look, Yanis...the deer!'

He looked across the landscape and over to a small clump of trees where there were some fallow deer. About twelve that he could see. A few of them were alert and keeping an eye out, whilst the others munched on grass. They were beautiful creatures. There were even two younger ones. Babies. What was the word? *Fawns?* They looked so sweet, with their large dark eyes.

To see them made him hopeful. Hopeful

that he would get to see his babies soon. See their eyes. Gaze into them. Adore them.

'You're smiling,' Sam said.

He laughed. 'Thinking happy thoughts.'

'Want to share them?'

'I was thinking of our babies. Holding them in my arms. Looking down at them. Falling in love with them. Do you ever think of that moment?'

She nodded. 'I do. Sometimes. When I allow myself to hope that everything will be all right.'

She stretched out her back, rubbed at it. He hoped she wasn't too uncomfortable. Carrying two babies, she was already the size of a singleton pregnancy at term, and it was affecting her centre of balance. And standing for long hours in surgery, slightly bent over an operating table, was doing nothing for her backache or her sore ankles.

'You okay?' Yanis asked.

'Fine—just stretching out a bit.'

'Want to sit for a bit? I've got a blanket.'

'Let's choose a good spot.'

They walked for about another ten minutes, just taking in the scenery. The quiet.

The blue skies. The sparrows and blackbirds and thrushes singing in the trees. Occasionally they heard a dog bark as it chased a Frisbee or a ball, a child's laughter. It was nice. Different from the beep of machines and the clank of instruments that they were so much more familiar with.

Eventually they found a spot near the Isabella Plantation, and Yanis laid out the blanket and opened up the basket of goodies. Once he and Sam both had plates of tiny sandwiches, strawberries and triangles of watermelon, they settled in to talk.

'How are you feeling regarding the possibility of ablation?' he asked.

She sighed, swallowing a bite of ham-and-cheese sandwich. 'I don't know. If it needs to be done, then it needs to be done, but... I don't enjoy the idea of being a patient under anaesthetic, increasing the risk of losing them and submitting my body to doctors again.'

'I understand that.'

'I think I'd feel better if you were in the theatre, too. Observing.'

'They wouldn't allow that. In this case, I'm

just the father. Being staff won't get me in the room.'

'It's the lack of control, I think, that worries me the most. What happened to me as a child made me feel powerless, and I vowed to never feel that way again.'

'There are moments when we all feel powerless. I feel it all the time just lately.'

'You do?' She looked at him almost hopefully, as if it reassured her to hear that.

'Of course! I can't do anything to help you. I can't stop the twins from being at risk of TTTS. I can't stop the fact that your placenta is low. That weighs on me more than you know.'

She smiled. 'Thank you.'

'For what?' He was confused.

'For confiding in me. For worrying. For trusting me enough to tell me.'

'We need to be honest with each other. You were honest with me about your past, about what happened to you. I can only hope to be the same.'

'You have something in your past you want to share?'

He smiled. *'Non.'*

He hoped he sounded convincing.

Since she'd told Yanis about her past, he'd been even more attentive—and she'd allowed him to take care of her. She was getting past the strangeness of someone being kind, and she was now trying to embrace the care and attention. And she found that even though she enjoyed it, she didn't want to take advantage.

She tried to look after him, too. Massaging his shoulders after a long surgery. Cooking him a meal most nights. Asking him out to see a movie. Bringing him hot drinks when he was busy and hadn't stopped to take a break.

She'd hoped he might expand on their conversation in Richmond Park. It had sounded, for a moment there, as if he had something in his past that he'd hoped to share, but then he had diverted the conversation. There was something. She was sure of it. But what? She had opened up to Yanis. Exposed herself. Made herself vulnerable in the attempt to bring them closer together. Why couldn't Yanis do the same? What was he hiding?

Otherwise the relationship they were developing was growing as quickly as her abdomen—and the weekly scans she'd been having were growing more and more concerning.

Her latest scan this morning had shown that there was beginning to be a sizeable difference between Twin B, the donor twin, and Twin A, the recipient twin. After her last surgery she had an appointment with her consultant, Mr Meyer, to see what he wanted to do. She knew laser ablation was an option, but she'd researched it and found that although it did work in a lot of cases, in some it didn't work at all, and in others, mothers lost one or both babies. It was a small minority, but it did happen, and that concerned her greatly.

But she had reached the magical twenty-four weeks of pregnancy now, so technically, if the twins had to be born early—even with all the possible complications of early delivery—they had a chance of survival.

She rubbed at her abdomen absently, smiling as the babies kicked, and hoped that she'd get to keep them inside her for a lot longer.

It was one thing to be a surgeon and be in control, knowing absolutely that what you were doing was right for your patient. It was completely another to be the patient and give yourself over into someone else's hands and hope that they knew what they were doing.

Of course, she'd researched Mr Meyer. She had done it the second she'd been assigned to him. He was a good doctor. A renowned obstetrician with a specialty in multiples and neonatal surgery. But it didn't matter how many gold stars he had against his name—this was *her* body, *her* babies. She might have thought that she felt scared as a child, submitting to all those procedures, but now she was terrified.

She was normally so great at hiding it, but now, with the TTTS getting worse, putting her babies at risk, she truly felt that maybe her mother had been right all along. Maybe her body couldn't carry babies without something going wrong. Maybe she was faulty and this situation was somehow all her own fault.

Yanis had told her she had to stop thinking that. Kept telling her it was simply bad luck. But what if it wasn't? She was terrified and the fear was all-consuming. She needed to know she could rely on Yanis, and she thought that she could, but there was something niggling away that she just couldn't put her finger on. Maybe he would tell her soon? Maybe he just needed a bit more time to feel that he could open up to her the way she had to him?

She wanted him to feel that he could tell her anything.

Because that way, when the worst happened—*if* it happened—then they'd both be able to get through it.

Mr Meyer looked grim.

Yanis did not like the look on his face at all, and he knew that significant news was coming.

'Your latest scan shows a considerable difference developing between the donor and recipient twins. My advice is that we schedule you for immediate laser ablation.'

Every word he delivered sank Yanis deeper

and deeper into fear. He'd hoped that this day would never happen. That it would not have come to this. But here they were, sitting in the consultant's office, being told that surgery was the only way forward if he and Sam wanted to keep their daughters inside the womb and healthy for a little while longer.

No one wanted to deliver these babies at twenty-four weeks. Not if they could help it. So surgery was the only option.

Yanis reached out and grasped Sam's hand, knowing that this news would terrify her. 'What will that entail exactly?'

But Yanis already pretty much knew. Like Sam, he had researched the surgery and knew the basics, but he wanted to hear from Mr Meyer just exactly how he hoped to approach the situation.

'Laser ablation is a minimally invasive surgery that will offer you the best chance at having two healthy babies. We perform it endoscopically, entering into the uterine sac of the recipient twin. We identify the cord insertion and follow the vessels that connect to the donor twin. This is where we bring in the laser and coagulate the vessels to ensure that there is no blood flow between the two twins. Next, we return to the sac of the recipient twin and drain fluid levels back to normal. Within about two weeks the urine output and fluid levels around both twins should have stabilised. We'll need you to rest afterwards. No working, Ms Gordon. No twelve-hour surgeries. I suggest you stay at home for three weeks.'

Sam nodded, but she seemed far away, in a world of her own. Yanis knew she had to be scared. Preparing herself to go under the knife once again. Something she hadn't done since childhood. It would most definitely bring back all those feelings of being helpless.

He felt helpless himself. In a situation in which he had no power. In which nothing he did would help at all. All he could do was support Sam and be strong for her and make sure that she followed doctor's orders. He would make sure of that.

'When will you do it?' he asked.

'First thing tomorrow morning. If you can get to the hospital for six, we could have you in Theatre by eight o'clock—how does that sound?'

They both nodded.

'We'll be there,' said Yanis, and looked to Sam. 'You go home, get ready, pack a small bag. I'll take care of your patients today and see if Ms Gupta can take over the scheduled surgeries for tomorrow.'

'Sure.'

He squeezed her hand tight and then looked at Mr Meyer. 'What are the risks of the procedure?'

'As doctors, you know that there is a risk with any surgical procedure. You need to fully understand that one or both of the babies might not survive. However, there are studies that show that babies treated with laser ablation are more likely to be free of neurological deficits than those who had only been treated with fluid reduction, and those who have the laser ablation generally remain in utero for longer than babies who don't have any surgical interference.'

'And the risk of the TTTS returning?'

'One study showed that the condition returned in fourteen out of a hundred and one pregnancies.'

'But *not* having the surgery puts the babies at risk?' Sam said.

'Unfortunately that is so. You also need to be aware of the risk of early rupture of the membranes. Having ablation might mean the rupture will happen within weeks of the surgery. There's also a risk of miscarriage and vaginal bleeding.'

'And the risk of infection,' Yanis added.

Mr Meyer nodded. 'It all sounds terribly grim, and I'm aware that it's not a wonderful choice that you're having to make. But in my opinion, if you want to have one or more babies by the time this pregnancy is over, then laser ablation is your best option. Despite all the risks.'

There seemed to be so much doom and gloom. They'd just have to hope that both babies made it through. That there were no complications. No infections. No loss of life.

Yanis turned and looked at Sam, knowing that if she got through this surgery he would do his damnedest to look after her and their girls. 'We'll do it. And I'll move in with Sam afterwards to make sure she rests.'

Sam opened her mouth as if to say something, but he stopped her.

'You have no choice in this matter. I'm going to look after you and you're going to like it. Okay?'

She seemed to think about that for a moment. Then she smiled and nodded as tears welled in her eyes. 'Thank you.'

Yanis sat next to Sam as she lay in her hospital bed, waiting to be taken down for her procedure. It was half past seven in the morning. As instructed, she'd had nothing to eat, only sips of water, after eight o'clock last night.

Sam had asked him to stay with her overnight at her flat, telling him that she didn't want to be alone the night before her procedure. That she needed someone to talk to her and keep her mind occupied whilst she waited.

But although they'd chatted about a variety of things, all Yanis could think about was those two girls inside her. His daughters. And the risk they were at. The risk Sam was at.

He'd got used to her. Used to having her by his side…used to the idea that they could be a family and that all his dreams just might come true. This hope that he felt welling inside, rising up out of his core, spreading throughout him, was agonising—because alongside it all was the doubt. The second-guessing. He couldn't lose them. Any of them.

Yanis struggled to internalise his feelings. Was this love? It was all frighteningly familiar. But although he desperately wanted to tell Sam what had happened in his past, he knew he couldn't do it right before this surgery. He couldn't put that extra worry on her—not right now.

If everything went well with the procedure and the babies were fine, then he'd say something. Because by then the TTTS would be fixed and they'd be in safer territory, knowing that even if their twins were born early they should be okay. Babies could survive if born after twenty-four weeks. It would be hard and a difficult road, but it was doable.

He'd tell her when she was recovered. When she was stronger. Because she *was* strong. Sam was strong. With all that she'd been through, look at how she'd come out on the other side of it. He admired her. More than she knew. For some people, stress and upset and heartache destroyed them, and they never recovered, but Sam…

He'd never realised the stress of holding in such a secret as his. And as he smiled at this woman he had come to care for a great deal, he wished he could take it all away for her. He'd happily take on that burden if it meant that Sam could be carefree again. He liked seeing her smile. He liked seeing her laugh. She'd not done much of that lately. She always seemed to be somewhere else. Distant. Her gaze unseeing, as if she was imagining the worst.

'It will be all right,' he said now, taking her hand and stroking it. 'Mr Meyer is the best and he knows what he's doing.'

She nodded. 'But this is *me*. Things tend to go wrong for me.'

Me too.

'We must be positive.'

'I know, but it's hard to be.'

'Maybe we should think of some names?'

She turned to look at him. 'Wouldn't that be tempting fate?'

He shook his head. 'No. It would be showing the world that we're not afraid to look forward. To plan. To hope for a good outcome. These girls—and you—are so precious to me. They're people already, no matter what happens, and I think they should have names.'

She smiled. 'I couldn't do this without you, Yanis.'

She reached up and stroked his face, and he leaned in for a gentle kiss.

'What about Yvette?' he asked.

She scrunched up her face. 'After your sister? What about Darcy?'

'It's a possibility. We should make a list.'

He got out his phone and brought up his notes app and typed in the name. 'Estelle?'

'Esme is nice. What about Addison?'

He smiled, relaxing somewhat. 'Charlotte? Isabella?'

He liked this. This moment of hope. He was lifting her. Supporting her. Showing her that what they were facing was possible. They could conquer it and come out on the other side. They only had to choose to believe it.

'Ms. Gordon? We're ready for you now.' A nurse stood at the end of the bed with a smile.

Sam turned to look at him. 'If anything happens...'

He got up, pressed his forehead to hers, holding her face in his hands. 'It won't.'

'You promise?'

He couldn't do that. He knew he couldn't. It was the one thing he couldn't promise and the one thing he wanted to promise more than anything.

The pain of keeping it in overrode logic. 'I promise.'

He dropped a kiss onto her lips and stood back as the nurse took hold of her bed and began to wheel her away.

He felt sick. Awful.

Feeling as if his future were being taken away from him, he stood there and watched.

Being helpless was the worst feeling in the whole entire world.

* * *

She dreamed she was young again. Lying in a hospital bed, her gown up over her stomach, while her mother sat by her bed, telling the doctors terrible things. Sam had something growing in her stomach—her mother was sure of it. She'd seen something move.

Sam was lying there frozen, unable to move, as the doctors stuck in big metal probes and moved them about. She could feel them doing something to her, but she couldn't stop it, so she began screaming and—

She woke slowly, blinking her eyes open to the sight of white ceiling tiles and fluorescent lights. There was the sound of a heart monitor...

Hospital. Right. She gazed down at her abdomen. *Still pregnant. Okay.* At the side of her bed sat a nurse, writing things down on a clipboard.

Sam licked her lips. Her mouth felt dry. As if she'd not had a drink for hours. What was the time? She felt her voice would be croaky. 'Hey...'

The nurse looked up and smiled, putting

the clipboard down on her chair. 'Hi. Your surgery went well and you're doing great.'

'It did? I am?' She felt relief surge through her—and then she fell asleep again. This time, thankfully, there were no bad dreams.

Much later she woke again, and this time she stayed awake.

The dark-haired nurse was smiling. 'Good, you're awake. We're about to take you back down to the ward.'

'Did everything go okay?'

She smiled. 'It went fine. Babies both doing very well.'

Sam felt reassured. At least for now. If the surgery had gone well, then that meant all she had to do was rest for a day or so in hospital, to recover from the surgery, then take bed rest at home for a couple of weeks. She could get back to work for a little bit longer before the babies arrived if all went well.

I hope so.

As the nurse wheeled her back onto the obstetrics ward, she saw Yanis get up from a chair and beam a smile at her. She felt her heart swell with happiness and joy to see him, and as she was wheeled into her bay, he took her hand and pressed his lips to it.

'*Sam.*'

'They say it went well, Yanis. We're all okay.' She felt so sleepy.

'I heard.' He bent over her and kissed her on the lips. 'How do you feel?'

'Bit tired…but I'm all right.'

'That's to be expected.'

'How long was I gone?'

'Too long. But you're back now, and it's good news, so all you need to do now is make sure you rest.'

Sam nodded. 'I'll try.'

'You will do more than try. And I'll make sure of it. Do you need a drink?'

'If there's any water, I'd love some.'

He passed her a plastic beaker with a straw in it and she took a few sips of iced water. The drink felt beautiful and cool upon her sore, dry throat, and she smiled her thanks afterwards.

'Are you okay?' she asked.

'I am now you're back. That was the longest wait of my entire life.'

'You don't have to stay with me now if you

need to go. I'm just going to be lying here for the next day or two.'

'I'm fine exactly where I am. I'll go when visiting is over—move some of my stuff to your place, so that I can look after you properly when you're out.'

'You're sweet.'

'Sweet?' He smiled. 'I'm sure you meant devoted. Or courageous? Or heroic? *Heroic* is a good word.'

They were very good words. But she had another one, too. 'Well, I'm thankful. Thankful that I have you. If I'd had to go through this on my own, I don't know how I'd have done it.'

He smiled, gazing softly into her eyes. 'You'd have rocked it. But you're not alone. Not with me. Do you understand? I will always be here for you. Always.'

It meant so much to her to hear those words, and the fact that she and the babies meant so much to him made her feel as if she wanted to say something similar back to him. But the words *I think I might love you* got stuck in her throat. She was too afraid to say them.

He'd probably think she was just strung out on anaesthetic, anyway, and that she wouldn't remember saying it. She wanted the first time she said that to someone to mean something. To be clear. To have no doubt about how much she meant it.

Besides, she was afraid to say it. She'd never said it to anyone. Never come close. And they seemed such huge words, with such power and intensity and meaning... She hesitated, because what if what she was feeling *wasn't* love? It could be infatuation, or something else. How would she know? She'd never experienced it before. She could just be confused.

And what if she said it and Yanis didn't feel the same way? That would be mortifying. Especially if he didn't say it back. Yanis might be saying all these wonderful things now, but what if he was just saying them because he was worried about the babies? About his two little daughters? And there was still the matter of Yanis holding back on something. Keeping something of himself back from her. She couldn't say *I love you* unless she felt she had every single part of him.

I'm racing ahead here.

Sam closed her eyes and allowed herself to drift in the fog of anaesthesia. It was easier there. She didn't have to face her feelings…her doubts, her fears, her confusion over Yanis. She didn't have to lie there thinking about how she was in hospital. A patient again. After surgery. And that something had been truly wrong with her this time.

Drifting was kind of blissful.

It meant she didn't have to face up to anything and confront it.

CHAPTER EIGHT

'OH, MY GOD, what's this?'

Sam laughed as Yanis walked into her bedroom carrying a tray. Upon the tray was a small vase with a mini bouquet of pink and purple flowers, a saucer with croissants and butter curls, a pot of strawberry jam, a plate of scrambled eggs and crispy bacon and a bowl of fresh fruit. Two glasses of freshly squeezed orange juice and a large cafetière of coffee.

'I can't eat all of that!'

'It's for both of us. I thought we could have a bed picnic for breakfast.'

'You're quite the picnic man, aren't you? I could get used to this.'

She let him plant a kiss upon her lips as he set the tray down on the bed and clambered on beside her. This last week or two at home with Yanis had been wonderful. He'd truly been the perfect carer. Bringing her breakfast every morning. Bringing her a cup of tea when she needed one and even when she didn't. Making her a fresh lunch or popping out to get her something she was craving. Cooking a homemade meal every night. He took care of the laundry, the shopping… He'd even assembled the buggy, when it arrived, and built the cots and sorted the nursery in her spare room at her exacting instructions.

He was considerate, caring, empathetic. He truly was the most wonderful man she had ever met. And every day her feelings for him became stronger and stronger.

The more time she spent with him, the more that they talked, and the more she wished she could say the words she was too scared to say. Three little words. But three words with such import, such deference, such power… She knew that, once said, they would change everything. They would move her and Yanis's relationship forward into territory where maybe Yanis did not want to go.

She believed that he felt the same way. At least, she hoped so. Why else was he here, looking after her so well?

And yet every time she had that thought,

asked that question, she heard her mother's voice in the back of her head telling her, *It's not you he's caring for... It's those babies.* Why was it that every time she had a doubt, that doubt spoke in the voice of her mother?

It couldn't be true, could it? Yanis seemed so genuine. So kind. She had never got the impression from him that he was caring for her only because of her role as incubator for his children.

But doubt still remained. The only time Sam had been important to other people was when she could give them something. To her mother, she had been a conduit for attention.

What if Yanis was only attending to her because he wanted the babies? More than he wanted her? What if he was leading her to believe that she was important so that he got what he wanted? His daughters. And then, once they were born, would she see less of him? Would he create a distance between them?

Sam was used to being used for other people's sakes. Her mother had used her, had even caused her harm, to get what she needed emotionally. And if her own mother could do that…

She bit into a croissant, ignoring the flakes of rich, buttery pastry that fell to the bedspread.

'Mr Meyer said you can start getting up today,' said Yanis. 'Moving around. I thought we could take a walk around the block…get you some fresh air?'

'That would be great. Being waited on hand and foot is wonderful, but cabin fever is not.'

He smiled. 'Why don't you freshen up and get dressed, whilst I clear all of this up?'

She nodded, and heard him clanking around in the kitchen as she got washed and dressed.

The sun was shining and summer had arrived. It would be nice to be outside.

He met her by the door, gave her a long, slow kiss that had her wishing they were heading back into the bedroom, rather than outside, and then took her hand and led her out.

They didn't go far. Just enough to do a bit of window shopping as she gazed adoringly at a shop filled with baby clothes, imagining dressing her own girls in all the pretty dresses she could see. Then they stopped at a small café and chose a table outdoors on the pavement.

A waitress came to get their order and they asked for lattes, still too full from breakfast to ask for anything to go with them.

'This is nice,' Sam said, sipping at her milky coffee.

'We should bring the girls here when they're older,' said Yanis. 'There's a children's area inside, filled with toys and books and a small ball pool.'

Sam smiled. 'It's nice to think of the future like that.'

'It is. And now you're through the surgery, there's no reason why we shouldn't think of it more often.'

'Do you think we're ready?'

'I hope so.'

She nodded and put down her mug. 'We haven't really spoken about the future. About when they're here. About how we'll share them.'

He looked away, across the road, watching

a mother push her child in a buggy. 'We'll find a way,' he said.

'We've got so close. You don't think that we ought to…?'

He glanced back at her. 'Ought to what?'

She shrugged. Embarrassed. *Move in to-gether?* They were practically living together now, and it was *so good*.

She sucked in a breath and made a less risky suggestion. 'Think about how we're going to fit in parenting around our work schedules.'

'I'm sure Elliot will be willing to work with us both.'

Sam nodded. 'He's a good man. And so are you.'

He smiled. *'Merci.'*

'You do know that if there's anything you want to tell me, you can? I want you to feel that I'm here as much for you as you seem to be for me.'

'I know.' He looked at her, as if thinking about saying something else, but then obviously decided against it.

She wondered what had passed through his mind, but said nothing as he got up and held out his hand to help her to her feet. As they continued their walk down the street, she wondered what it was that bothered him. Something did, and she was terrified that it was something huge—that she had read him wrong.

Because she was really falling in love with Yanis, and if it wasn't reciprocated, she could see herself getting very hurt indeed.

'I just think it's time I faced the truth head-on. I can't keep going like this.'

Martin Merriweather, Yanis's private patient, sat in front of him, his tremors plainly visible. It was clear that he had reached his limit, and from his movements, Yanis felt sure that Mr Merriweather wouldn't even be able to sit and hold his own cup of tea without a spillage occurring. And the tremors weren't just in his hands. His bottom lip quivered, and he walked with a hunched gait, as if he couldn't lift his feet off the floor properly.

'Surgery is a big step, Martin. You're definitely sure you want to proceed?'

His patient leaned forward. 'My wife and I

want to renew our vows. We've set the date for next year. We're going to have a big ceremony. Make up for the small registry office thing we had forty years ago. Our children are going to be there. Our grandchildren. And I, for one, would like to walk my wife down the aisle without looking like I'm being electrocuted.'

Yanis nodded. 'I understand.'

'These tremors are getting beyond a joke, Doctor. They affect everything. Surgery has always been my last resort option, and I'm there. I want to try the deep brain stimulation. I'd like to have my last few final years with control of my body. Is that too much to ask?'

'Of course not. But before we allow you to have DBS, we have to assess you for a period of months, both on and off your medication. You'll also need an MRI. It's procedure. But if we find you're a suitable candidate, we can proceed.'

Yanis typed on his keyboard and then turned the screen around so that Martin could see a diagram of what happened during surgery.

'Okay. So, if you meet the criteria, what we do is this: we insert a pulse generator— it's a bit like a pacemaker—under the skin in your chest area. That generator is connected to some very fine wires that are inserted into specific areas of your brain that allow motor control. Do you see here?'

Yanis pointed out the various parts on screen.

Martin nodded.

'We switch on the generator and the electrodes deliver high-frequency stimulation to the area that is targeted. This stimulation changes the electrical signals in your brain that cause the symptoms of your disease.'

'Like jump leads for a car?'

'Sort of. But if you definitely want to proceed down this path, I must reiterate the fact that this surgery is not a cure, and it won't stop your Parkinson's from progressing.'

'I know.'

'But it should give you better control of your movements.'

'Good. That's good. You don't realise what you miss doing... I can't even sign my own name. Can you imagine how that feels?'

Yanis nodded. 'I can imagine the difficulties. But, as with all surgery, there are risks involved. Bleeding. Stroke. And you'll have to consider whether you will be able to cope with the part of surgery when we wake you to check your movements.'

'I'd be *awake* for the surgery?'

'*Oui.*'

'With my skull open?'

Yanis smiled. '*Oui.*'

'Okay... What else?'

'You'll need to stay in hospital afterwards for a few days—to recover, and also so that we can monitor your stimulator settings and adjust your medication so that you get the most benefit from your surgery.'

'Okay, Doc, so how do I proceed?'

'You definitely want to go ahead?'

'I do.' Martin smiled, as if already imagining himself at the altar next to his wife.

Yanis nodded. 'All right. So, I shall write to your GP, instructing him on how we wish to do the assessment first. You're currently on your medication, so I'll want you to keep a diary for a couple of weeks, detailing what your tremors are like, what difficulties you're having, what things you are able to do by yourself. After that we will discuss how to safely take you off your medication. Obviously at this point your wife will have to keep the diary for you, if you have difficulty writing or typing. Then we'll schedule your MRI and look at all the results. If you're a candidate, we'll make an appointment for surgery.'

'Thank you, Doctor.'

When his patient had gone, Yanis found himself thinking about Martin Merriweather. The man had been through enough and decided he needed to face the truth of his situation and try to make it better. Medication had helped mask his symptoms for a while, but the truth of a situation always came to the fore.

Yanis knew that he had to do the same thing with Sam. He'd kept his secret for far too long and she was doing well now. The babies had made it through the ablation surgery and Sam was looking forward to returning to work. Surely they were all safe now? Surely now he could tell her about his past? About Giselle and the babies he had lost before?

He cared for Sam deeply. More than cared. It was possible that he loved her.

She was difficult sometimes, prickly on occasion, but he understood her. Worried about her. Enjoyed being with her. Looking at her smile lit up his life. Seeing her happy made him happy. When he wasn't with her, he found himself thinking of her and wondering what she was doing. He liked waking up with her. He liked going to bed with her. She was carrying his twin daughters and he could foresee a wonderful future for them all.

He'd missed being a part of something. Part of a family. Being with Sam gave him that feeling back, and he didn't want to lose it.

But he couldn't go into the future with his secret, and if he was going to give all of himself to Sam then she had to know him.

All of him.

Including his sad history.

Resolute, he decided to head for home.

Sam had laid the table for two. Ideally, she would have liked to go all out and really decorated the table—looked for a tablecloth, hunted down some long candles, maybe a small bouquet of flowers…

But instead of heading out to the florist's and picking up something special, she'd re-used the small bouquet that Yanis had included on her breakfast tray that morning. And, unable to go out and hunt down a fabulous lunch, she'd opened a couple of tins of soup and warmed some part-baked bread in the oven.

He would be home soon, and Sam was hoping that she could take the opportunity to talk about them and where they were heading, what their future would look like. By sounding him out on those issues, she'd be able to gauge where he was, and if she could finally say to him those magic words she dreamed of saying.

She pictured the look on his face when she said it. The way his eyes might light up…the way a smile might creep across his face. The way he might reach across the table to take her hand in his and whisper *I love you, too.*

If that happened… She couldn't imagine how happy she'd be. To have found someone like him. Someone who knew her history.

Who really understood her, and loved her, and wanted to be in her life for ever.

They could have the dream. And why shouldn't she wish for it? Hadn't she already been through so much suffering? Eventually someone like her had to have some good luck, right?

She heard his key in the lock and felt her heart race at the thought of what she was going to say. She simply couldn't allow the thought that he might say nothing back.

These last couple of weeks since the surgery had shown her how much he cared. A man simply didn't do as much as he was doing for a woman if he didn't care deeply for her. She meant something to him—Sam was sure of it. And now she really wanted them to move forward, towards the birth of the twins, knowing exactly where they stood with one another.

Turning down the heat on the soup, she sat at the kitchen table, a smile upon her face.

He came in, carrying a folder or two, and put them down on the hall table. 'Something smells nice. Have you been cooking? I told you not to do anything,' he admonished gently as he came into the kitchen and saw her sitting there.

He walked over and cupped her face, kissing her lightly on the lips.

'It's just some tinned soup. Hardly a roast dinner. How did it go with your patient?'

'We're going to do the assessment to see if he's a candidate for DBS.'

'Well, fingers crossed he is. Why don't you sit down and let me look after you for a change?'

Yanis shook his head. 'No, you stay seated. I'll finish it off. Is that bread in the oven?'

'Yes. It should be ready, if you're hungry.'

'Starving. What drink do you want with your meal?'

'Just tea would be great.'

Butterflies were swirling in her stomach. But they were so good together. The domestic set-up worked for them both. She was happy to have Yanis in her home and he *fitted*. They were perfect together.

The urge to blurt out what she wanted to say was incredibly strong, but she thought they should eat first.

Yanis served up the meal, and soon they

were both tucking into French onion soup. It was beautiful with the warm crusty bread and, despite her nerves, Sam devoured everything.

As she sipped her tea, she decided to broach the subject. 'So, I can go back to work soon. Things are moving on… There haven't been any problems with the twins… I feel great. Strong. I guess we really need to start looking towards the future.'

He nodded. 'I guess we do.'

'I've really enjoyed having you here with me, Yanis. I wouldn't have been able to do it without you.'

'It's been my pleasure. It's been good for us.'

'It has.'

Was this her moment? The now or never?

But Yanis spoke first. 'I've been wanting to talk to you, actually.'

'Oh?'

Perhaps she wouldn't have to be the one to put herself out there. Perhaps Yanis was going to do it first?

Relief flooded through her and she beamed, looking at him. Trying to show him that she was ready to hear it. Ready to hear what he had to say and that she'd *welcome* it. She was encouraging him to say what he needed to say. She'd told him before that he could tell her anything.

'I've been wanting to do it, but I wanted to wait for the right time.'

He seemed nervous. She could understand that. She was nervous, too. So she did what she'd expected *him* to do. She reached out and took his hand.

'You can tell me anything,' she said.

This was it. She felt it. The crucial moment when he would tell her what had been bothering him, and then she would know, and it would be nothing at all, and they could skip into the future as a happy couple.

At least, she hoped so.

Yanis gave a quick, nervous smile. 'Okay. I guess I can, now that you're better. Now that you're stronger. Now that everything has gone so well.'

She laughed. He was making her nervous now. 'What is it?' she asked.

He bit his lip, squeezed her hand and let out a breath. 'I used to be married.'

What? She heard the words, but they were so unexpected, so out of the blue, that at first she didn't quite understand them.

'Married?' She pulled her hand free of his. Shocked.

'*Oui*. Giselle and I had known each other since school. We were great friends first, before we fell in love.'

Sam's stomach churned. *Giselle*. The name itself sounded so beautiful and exotic—as if she was someone Sam could never, ever dream of comparing herself with without losing.

'We got married as soon as we could. It seemed silly to wait. We had already been together all those years—we wanted to get married and start a family as soon as we could.'

Start a family?

A deep, dark sense of dread began in Sam's stomach and she suddenly wished she'd not eaten all that food.

Yanis had been married before.

'Giselle got pregnant just as I got into medical school...'

Yanis's gaze was fixed on a distant object. As if it was safer for him to look some-where else other than into Sam's eyes. As if he didn't want to see her reaction. As if the act of her pulling her hand free of his had told him that they weren't as close as he'd hoped.

'We were both ecstatic and we told every-one we knew. But then she lost the baby a couple of weeks after.'

Sam stared at him, imagining that loss. 'I'm sorry,' she whispered. They were the only words she could squeeze out of her tight, locked-down throat.

'We were both hit hard by the loss, as I'm sure you can imagine, but we knew that mis-carriage was unfortunately common with first pregnancies, and so after some time we decided to try again.'

Sam's heart was thudding hard. Every beat was a painful knock inside her chest. She could feel herself growing hot. Could feel her legs becoming shaky and was not sure she wanted to hear any more of this.

'She got pregnant again, and this time we were more cautious. We decided not to tell anybody until she'd got to twelve weeks and we'd had a scan. She seemed fine. We thought everything was going well. Until they told us at the scan that they couldn't find a heartbeat.'

Sam closed her eyes, imagining the horror of that sort of thing happening to them. How did you get past something like that?

'She had a D&C and both of us were broken into pieces.'

Sam rubbed at her belly with her free hand, glad that she could feel her own babies kicking and moving.

'We were hit hard, and we dealt with it in different ways. I worked harder. Giselle retreated into herself. She saw doctors who told us that we weren't exceptional, that we just needed to keep trying.'

'What happened?'

She didn't want to hear the answer, but she *needed* to hear how this ended.

Now he looked at her, imploring her with his eyes to understand.

'We'd had all these dreams of becoming a family. Dreams of what that might be like. I wanted us to try again, but I knew I had to wait for Giselle to want the same thing and not put pressure on her. Eventually she began talking about trying for one last time. But she said that if this one didn't work out, then she didn't know what we'd do. We began trying and she fell pregnant once again.'

Sam realised she was holding her breath and had to force herself to breathe.

'Once again we were quietly cautious, quietly happy. We didn't dare to hope. But at the first scan everything went well, and we finally began to believe that we would be okay. We told everyone and, like us, they were cautiously optimistic.'

Sam saw the grief in him, saw it so openly laid bare, and realised that all this time with her he must have been so scared that they were going to lose the babies. Suddenly her heart melted into a puddle at his pain. She wanted to scoop him up into her arms and hold him tight and never let him go. But she couldn't.

'Then, at thirty weeks, she realised she couldn't feel the baby moving. We rushed to the hospital and they told us that the baby had died.'

'Oh, Yanis…' She couldn't stop herself.

She got up and went around to his side of the table. He stood and she took him in her arms, shocked to feel him trembling.

'I so wanted to tell you!' His voice broke. 'But I couldn't. I didn't want to terrify you—not when you were already so scared about what might happen. I kept it inside…to protect you.'

Now she understood. How scared he must have been! And all this time she'd thought that only she could truly imagine how it might all go wrong for them.

She took his hand and walked with him over to the couch. Sat him down. 'What happened then?' she asked.

'Giselle had to give birth. They induced her, and she had to go to a special suite for mothers whose babies were stillborn. But we could still hear other mothers with their perfectly healthy babies in other rooms. And every time we heard a baby cry out, it broke us.'

'I don't know what to say…'

'We had a little boy. We named him Jacques. We got to be with him for a while, but eventually we had to let him go. Then we went home and tried to grieve.'

Sam wiped her eyes. This was unimaginable. To think Yanis had held all this inside him... He must have been so scared. No wonder he hadn't told her.

'But losing Jacques broke us apart. I tried to be there for Giselle, but whatever I did was not enough. I wanted to be with her, talk to her, comfort her. But every time I tried to touch her she'd flinch. She dealt with her grief by retreating. Every time I went near her she turned away from me. Like she didn't want me near her...like she blamed me.'

'I'm so sorry.'

'We split up eventually, and I knew I could never go through all that again.'

She nodded. 'Until *I* got pregnant?'

'*Oui.*'

Sam felt awful for everything he'd been through. She wanted to comfort him, but she was reeling from all this information.

The conversation had not gone as she'd been expecting, but now was not the time to say what she'd wanted to say. Plus...she wasn't sure if she even could now.

This was a huge secret. Something Yanis had kept to himself throughout the entire time she had known him. What else might there be? What else didn't she know about him? Were there any more secrets lurking in his past?

It made Sam feel that maybe she didn't know Yanis as well as she'd thought. Maybe she'd had a lucky escape in not saying anything. Maybe she needed to take some time to get to know Yanis more.

She wished that he had told her before—but she was also glad that he hadn't told her. If she'd known about it in advance, she would have been even more terrified about something going wrong with the pregnancy.

The dilemma was confusing.

All of this was confusing.

And now she didn't know how to feel.

But she did want to be there for him the way he had been there for her throughout all this.

Sam laid her head upon his shoulder. He'd said he hadn't ever wanted to go through all this again and look what had happened. Did he just mean the pregnancy? Or becoming a father? Or did he mean more? Becoming a husband? A 'significant other' in a relationship?

'I felt like I'd failed my wife. That I hadn't been able to protect her. That I hadn't been able to stop her from getting hurt. I blamed myself after she left.'

'It wasn't your fault. You weren't to know what would happen.'

'I was so scared when you went in for surgery. I wasn't sure I could stand it. It was one of the most terrible waits in my entire life.'

'But we got through it.' She lifted her head and turned to look at him, tears in her eyes. 'We're okay. We're good.'

He raised her hand to his lips and kissed it. 'I know. Do you see now why I needed to be here to look after you?'

'I do.'

'I want to be here all the time, Sam. I know I have my own place—I know that. But being here with you every day… To go back to my own place now, after all of this, would make me feel…lost.'

'What are you saying? Are you asking to move in permanently?'

She almost didn't dare to think about it. The Sam she'd been before his revelation would have welcomed it, but the Sam she was now had some reservations. She loved him, yes, but he'd blown her out of the water with this. She needed time to think. She needed time to take it all in. He'd kept this massive secret from her and...

She felt ashamed for her next thought.

What if Giselle hadn't left him but he'd left her? To find someone who could give him the family he wanted?

She shook her head to clear the thought from it. No. That couldn't have happened.

'I want to be with you,' he said.

Sam nodded. Unsure what else to do. She could hardly kick him out and say no right now.

'Let's take it one day at a time, huh?'

Yanis smiled and kissed her. 'One day at a time sounds perfect.'

Standing in the car park, looking up at the hospital, Sam felt that her stomach was full of butterflies.

'Nervous?' Yanis held her hand.

Yes. And not just about this.

'Yeah, it feels strange to be back. I want to work—I do. I just feel like there's going to be a lot of questions. Maybe I can hide out in clinic all day.'

Yanis laughed. 'You don't have to go in if you don't want to. You could start early maternity leave. I'd support you in that.'

He'd said that before. But his need to wrap her in cotton wool seemed overpowering to her now, rather than nurturing. She couldn't get the thought out of her head that he might only be interested in the babies.

'We've already discussed this. Me staying at home would be a nightmare solution. I'd go crazy without a scalpel in my hand. Without being in Theatre. Being a neurosurgeon is who I am.' She turned to look at him. 'I'm fine. Mr Meyer has given me the all-clear and I'm back now.'

'Just remember to take it easy. You're nearly eight months pregnant with twins. I want to see you eating and drinking and, most importantly, sitting down whenever you get the opportunity.'

'You don't have to babysit me, Yanis. I'm a grown woman.'

Was Yanis just desperate to start a family? To replace what he had lost? Maybe he'd never expected to start a family with her, but it had happened, so he was making the best of it?

She hated having these invasive thoughts. Because everything about him screamed that he was nothing like that. Only he'd lost so much… And she could imagine that if she'd been the one to lose three babies, having another baby would be the only thing on her mind.

'Indulge me,' he said.

He kissed her, and she allowed herself to sink into it. To enjoy the pleasure of his touch. Because what if all this was fleeting? What if it went away the second the girls arrived?

She hated feeling needy, but she was hormonal and scared. And she was feeling enormous now. Nothing fitted very well, she always felt her ankles hurting by midday, and if she ate anything she got heartburn.

But she knew that if she got the chance to

get inside Theatre, then all of that would go away. With a scalpel in her hand, she could make the outside world disappear while she fixed someone's brain or spine. She needed that much more than she needed to be sitting at home watching cookery shows, waiting for her contractions to start.

She'd come such a long way. It was hard to think that at the beginning of this she'd hated the idea of becoming a mother. Had feared it. But with Yanis at her side, she had grown. He had helped her see that she could be anyone she wanted to be. They'd both been through some terrible times, but the future looked bright for both of them now. All they had to do was keep it together.

Maybe the babies arriving would make everything better? Maybe the doubts would go away and she would see Yanis as the perfect partner again?

Because he was. He'd shown her no reason to believe that her fears were real. This was all coming from inside her own mind. Her own suspicions. Because she'd been used before. By her own mother. The finishing line for them both was so close now…she could soon have everything she wanted!

Yanis seemed brighter since sharing his burden. He smiled more. Laughed more. He really seemed to be enjoying the time he spent with her and she loved being in his company. But there was still something… An edge. A sharp edge that cut her if she tried going near it. The babies weren't here yet. They weren't completely out of danger. Anything could happen. Who knew? Yanis had thought his son Jacques was out of danger and look what had happened there.

Since he'd told her, Sam had been almost militant in ensuring she could feel her babies moving. She took the time to notice. She counted movements. Made sure she felt more than ten every day, panicking whenever she only felt kicks in one place, thinking something had happened to one of the twins, but not the other.

Yanis had had such awful luck with pregnancies in the past. What if there was something fundamentally wrong with both of them?

Would she relax once the babies were born?

Maybe. All she'd have to worry about then was SIDS, or meningitis, or a whole host of other terrible things.

Wow. Parenting is one long worry.

She saw her friend Gil talking to a patient in a wheelchair over by the entrance and gave him a wave. He waved back as they went over to the lifts and pressed the button that would take them up to the neuro floor.

'You've got your outpatient clinic first?'

Yanis's question brought her thoughts back to the present.

She nodded. 'Yeah. It's a light day—half as many patients as usual. Sonja has followed my instructions not to fill my diary this first week, so I should be done by midday if any emergent surgeries happen.'

Sonja was her secretary.

'And if there's any problem you'll call me—for anything.'

She smiled. 'I will. You're in surgery?'

'*Oui.* Pituitary tumour removal up first, I believe.'

The lift doors pinged open and they walked their separate ways.

'Sam?' Yanis turned around.

'Yes?'

'Take it easy.' He grinned and blew her a kiss.

Automatically she reached out to catch it, then felt silly. But who cared? No one else was around, and she actually quite liked the way he looked out for her.

Sam pressed the kiss to her face and, determined to think good thoughts, headed to her morning clinic.

As Yanis successfully removed the pituitary adenoma on his patient, he let out a sigh of relief. Hopefully now his patient would suffer fewer headaches and get back the peripheral vision that he was losing.

'You wouldn't think it would matter, Doc. Not being able to see the stuff that you wouldn't normally notice. But when it's gone…when you don't have it any more… you realise how important it was and how much you want it back.'

He sympathised. Of course he did. He was missing so many of the simple things in life whilst he was worrying about Sam. Not being able to tell her his secret, fretting all the time, needing to know she was okay, making sure she wasn't having any weird symptoms. He was so focused on Sam he couldn't see anything else. He had tunnel vision. Only making sure Sam and the babies were okay.

Having told her everything, he felt as if a weight had been lifted a little. Not totally. Since telling Sam, she'd been…a little different towards him. Not hugely different, but it was almost as if he felt she was looking at him in a strange way…a considering way— as if she was trying to make her mind up about something.

He'd been so scared of telling her about Giselle, hoping she wouldn't freak out. She hadn't done that, but still something was off and he couldn't work out what it was. He didn't want to smother her with his feelings for her, so he was trying to give her space. Time to process all that he had told her. But it was hard to take a step back.

He liked being with her. *His Sam*. Beautiful, wonderful Sam. He liked her delicate hands. The way she moved, even heavily pregnant. She looked *good*. Those things had always been there, but his mind was focused so intently on keeping Sam and the babies safe that he'd almost stopped noticing them.

It had happened with Giselle, too—especially with that last pregnancy. Of course Giselle had pushed him away, accused him of suffocating her, of not giving her a moment's peace, and he'd tried to learn from that. He'd tried not to suffocate Sam and give her space and opportunity without constantly being there...hovering. It was hard, but he was doing it. Giving space to the woman he loved when all he wanted to do was be there for her and protect her and keep her safe. When all he wanted was to be stuck to her side like a limpet?

He smiled. They'd get through it. They were stronger than they'd ever been, and although he'd not really wanted her to return to work, he'd known he had to take a step back and let Sam make the choice. It was her body. Her life. And she was a grown woman, intelligent and creative and beautiful. He had to show her that he trusted her.

After all, she would be in the right place—a hospital—if help was needed, and at work he could keep an eye on her still. Not because he didn't trust her. He did. Implicitly. It was just that she was so near the end of her pregnancy now, and labour could start at any time.

It was difficult at night time, when they lay in bed together. He would spoon her, inhale her scent, his nose nestled in her hair. He'd hold on to her, and his body would want to do all the wonderfully delightful naughty things he could think of. But sex had been taken off the agenda since the ablation. It had seemed the safe thing to do and neither of them wanted to break that, no matter how turned on they got.

He missed that intimate connection, but he knew they'd get it back.

He just had to be patient.

He just had to wait.

And if this pregnancy had taught him anything, it had taught him to be patient.

CHAPTER NINE

HER MORNING CLINIC went smoothly. She was able to sit for most of it and just talk to her patients—check to see how they were doing post-surgery and post-rehabilitation. These were the clinics she really enjoyed, seeing the progress her patients had made, how their lives were different—how much she and her entire team had helped change a life.

On occasion there were patients who still had some difficulties, but they were getting there, adapting to a new situation and accepting a new normal. They inspired her. Made her see that if they could overcome great individual barriers and move beyond them to complete things they'd never thought possible, then so could she.

This pregnancy had changed her so much, and beyond that, Yanis had helped her grow, too. She was contemplating being a mother without fear, feeling that she had the power within her to do it, and that together they were strong. And now they were *so close* to the finishing line.

They met for lunch in the hospital cafeteria, and she was just contemplating going home early when she was paged by Accident and Emergency to consult on a case.

'Let me take it,' Yanis said. 'You go home and get some rest.'

'It's fine, honestly. I've been sitting all day. It'll do me good to waddle down there. Let me go and see what the case is, and if it's surgical then I'll let you take it.'

He nodded. 'All right.'

She headed down to A & E and was directed to Majors, where she was told about an elderly gentleman called Edward Forster. She went to see him and found him lying in bed with a middle-aged woman sitting beside him.

'Hello, I'm Samantha Gordon. You must be Mr Forster?'

The man just looked at her.

'He can't speak. We think he's had a stroke,' said the woman.

'Are you family?'

'No. I'm Sylvie. I work at a dog rescue centre and Edward is a volunteer with us. He walks the dogs.'

'And can you tell me what happened today, Sylvie?'

As Sam performed her examination on Edward, Sylvie explained what had happened.

'He'd just come back from walking Duke and was putting him back into his kennel when he suddenly seemed a bit unsteady. When I got to him he was slumped on the ground and his face looked odd. I did that FAST thing you see on that advert on television, and it seemed to show he'd had a stroke.'

Sam agreed. Her own FAST assessment on Edward—checking his face to see whether it had fallen on one side, seeing whether or not Edward could raise both arms and keep them there, what his speech was like—had made it clear that Edward was experiencing an event.

'What time was this exactly?'

'About twelve-thirty.'

Sam nodded. Edward's face had a slight droop to the left side, his left hand could not be raised as high as the right and seemed weaker in its grip, and he had aphasia. She needed to get him to a CT scan immediately. It would tell them if Edward had had an ischaemic stroke, caused by a blocked artery in the brain, or a haemorrhagic stroke, caused by a burst blood vessel.

'Do you know if he has any other medical problems?' she asked.

'I don't… Sorry.'

'I'm going to get him to CT. If you've got any contact details for his family, you should call them—or give the numbers to the nurse and she can do it for you.'

Sylvie nodded. 'Will he be all right?'

'We'll do our best for him.'

She could never promise that a patient would be one hundred per cent recovered, because she just didn't know. Sam could operate on hundreds of stroke victims and the results would all be different. There would be successes and failures. And although relatives and friends just yearned to have confirmation that everything would be all right, she could not promise anything except to do her very best.

Sam left to order the CT, and then asked a nurse to page Yanis. She wanted him available if surgery was needed.

When the CT scan results came in and showed that Edward was having a haemorrhagic bleed in his brain that would need surgery, she phoned Neurosurgery and told them to prep Theatre for a craniotomy.

Then she called Yanis. 'Are you free to complete the surgery?'

'Sure. No problem. I'll be there in a minute.'

'I'll meet you there.'

Yanis was gowned and gloved and ready when she saw him next.

'Look after him,' she told him. 'He's a good guy. Volunteers at a dog shelter. We need people like him.'

'I will. Are you going home?'

'I thought I'd wait and see how the surgery goes. You'll come find me when it's done?'

'*Oui.*' Yanis headed into Theatre and for a brief moment she watched him from the scrub room, wishing that she was in there. Maybe she'd do the next surgery that came along? She ached to get back to it.

Sam went to her office and caught up on a bit of paperwork, dictated a couple of letters to be sent to GPs. Just when she thought she ought to check on how Yanis was getting on in surgery, her pager went off. She was needed yet again in Accident and Emergency.

She headed down in the lift, rubbing at her abdomen as her girls happily kicked and stretched as if they were doing some sort of twin yoga workout, and arrived in A & E to find the doctors swarming around a teenage girl.

From the doctor leading the case, she discovered that the seventeen-year-old had been cycling on her way home from college, without a helmet, and had been hit by a car and flung over the bonnet, landing on the road head-first. She was unconscious, and bleeding from multiple contusions.

Sam pushed to the head of the table to do a neuro exam and it was soon clear that there was some head trauma. Not just from the gaping gash that had been bandaged by the paramedics, but also from the evidence of a blown pupil.

'Let's get her to CT—stat.'

Sam stepped back and allowed the team to rush the young girl—Jahira Stevens—to the scanning department. They needed to get her into surgery quickly. Every second counted, but she couldn't afford to operate blind. She needed to know what was going on.

'Page Mr Baptiste and find out how much longer he'll be in surgery, then tell him to meet me in Theatre Two.'

As the scan images came in, Sam could see that Jahira had a massive bleed on the right side of her brain and that they would need to go in and evacuate the clot.

She'd not planned on doing any surgery today. By rights, she should be at home by now, resting. But she was glad that she was here to help this young girl, who still had all her future in front of her and, if Sam was quick, would hopefully get through this trauma with all her faculties. Her neck was clear, so they didn't have to worry about paraplegia. All Sam had to do was fix this girl's brain.

As she scrubbed in the scrub room, she felt the adrenaline begin to surge, as it always did when she was about to do a surgery. The feeling was familiar, and welcome, and it made her feel as if she was truly back. Back to being the Samantha Gordon she knew she could be.

Confident. Clear-headed. In control.

Yanis pulled off his scrub cap and mask, signing the chart for a nurse as he did so. 'Let's get Mr Forster to neuro ICU. I want hourly obs—all right?'

'Yes, Doctor.'

As he started to scrub, his pager went off, and he pulled it from his pocket and frowned. A page to A & E?

He grabbed the nearest phone and discovered that another neuro case had come in and Sam had taken the patient to Theatre Two. He was to scrub in, when he could.

He quickly washed his hands. This other case meant that Sam must have gone into Theatre, which was slightly worrying. He hadn't wanted her doing any surgeries on her first day back. Surgeries were stressful and exhausting, even if at the time they felt as if they were energising you. He'd hoped that Sam would be resting by now. That she would be sitting with her feet up, sipping a hot cup of tea.

He should have known she would have taken this case straight away.

In Theatre Two, he rescrubbed and put on a fresh gown and mask. A nurse helped him on with his gloves as he walked through.

'What have we got?' he asked.

'Seventeen-year-old cyclist versus car,' said Sam. 'Blew her pupil, so I got her straight in. I've performed a craniotomy and I'm currently evacuating the clot.'

'Like me to assist?'

Sam looked up at him and her eyes creased, indicating a smile. 'Yes, please.'

He stood opposite her and helped provide gauze and suction. 'Nasty. Was she wearing a helmet?'

Sam sighed. 'No, unfortunately.'

'She could have saved herself a whole heap of trouble if she had been.'

'I'm sure everyone will tell her that when we get her into Recovery. This might just have been a one-off. Maybe she was in a rush and forgot to pick up her helmet. Maybe she usually wears one but something today made her forget. We can't judge her. We don't know.'

'Well, I'm going to damn well make sure that *our* girls wear helmets,' he said with passion.

Sam looked up at him. 'Oh, so you're going to be one of those fathers? Overprotective. A helicopter parent.'

He'd never heard that English phrase before. 'What does that mean?'

'It means you'll hover over them, paying close attention to their every move.'

He smiled at the image. 'You say that like it's a bad thing.'

Sam laughed. 'No. In fact, I like it. I love the fact that you want to protect them so much. It's nice. It's refreshing...'

'I hear a "but" coming...'

'But we won't be able to protect them from everything. At some point we'll both have to let go and trust them to do the right thing.'

'That's years away. For now, let me be a helicopter dad.'

She laughed. 'Okay.'

With the clot fully evacuated and the bleed stopped, Sam sighed and bandaged up the patient's head. 'Her brain has significant swelling. We can't put the skull flap back until it goes down a bit. Let's give her twenty-four hours and then we can bring her back in to complete the surgery.'

'All right.'

Sam had suddenly gone very still.

'Sam? Are you okay?' he asked.

She didn't look at him. She just continued to stare down before calmly handing her instruments to the nurse at her side. Then she took a step back and sucked in a breath.

Something was wrong. He knew it. All his instincts were aroused. 'Sam?'

'Er... Ms Gordon?' A scrub nurse spoke from behind Sam. 'I don't want to alarm you, but...you're bleeding....'

Yanis rushed around to the other side of the table to look at Sam. She stood there in pale blue scrubs and gown, but the bottoms were stained with red. A bright, alarming red that continued to spread as she bled actively.

'Nurse, take Jahira to recovery,' he said frantically.

And then he rushed to catch Sam before she fell.

* * *

'Yanis, what's happening?'

Sam lay on a trolley, being pushed rapidly through the corridors towards another theatre. Her heart was pounding so hard, so fast, she thought she might pass out. And she felt so weak. So fragile. And the look on Yanis's face was one of the utmost fear.

'Are the babies okay?'

She had to know. Had to know that she hadn't done anything wrong. Was this placenta praevia? Was the placenta tearing away from the uterine wall? Because if it was, then she could lose the twins, and she'd come too far to lose them now.

'I don't know. I've paged Obstetrics.'

'We need Mr Meyer.'

'I've paged whoever is free.'

'Yanis, we can't lose them. This isn't fair! I had the surgery. I did everything right. This isn't my fault!'

'It's no one's fault.'

'You told me we could do this. You said we'd be okay!'

'We will be.'

They turned a corner and her trolley bashed

its way through the double doors that led into the pre-theatre room. It was normally where they anaesthetised their patients and made sure they were stable before taking them through to surgery.

Were they going to put her out?

They couldn't do that!

She needed to know they were okay.

Sam tried to sit up, but Yanis pushed her down.

'What are you doing? I need to—'

'Sam! Lie down! I need you to stay still.'

But she couldn't. Panicking now, she remembered going in for all those surgeries as a child. When they'd wheeled her through and her mum had had to let go of her and leave her in the hands of the doctors. She'd been so scared. She'd always tried to get up, but hands had pushed her back down, a mask had been placed over her face...

She'd felt herself losing control. Felt the fear, the horror of what was going to happen... She was about to be cut open... Someone would be rummaging around inside her when she didn't want it, didn't need it. There had been helplessness, hopelessness. No power to stop what was happening…

It all came flooding back now and Sam struggled, fought to get off the trolley. But she was too weak, too ineffectual to stop the hands that were holding her down. Yanis was holding her down. She wanted to stop him. Wanted to make him let go.

'This is *your* fault! I can't believe you're doing this to me. *You* made this happen. This is all your fault!'

'Sam—'

'I never wanted this. I never felt I could do this. But you told me! You told me I could do it. I knew I was broken, I knew I was faulty, and so did you! We were doomed from the start—both of us!'

'Sam!'

She pulled herself free of him. 'Admit it! You've only stayed because of the babies. Giselle didn't walk away from you—you walked away from *her*! When she couldn't give you a child!'

Yanis stared at her, shock written across his face.

Did that mean it was true?

Behind her, she heard the doors open and a familiar man's voice. Mr Meyer? And then he was there, pushing forward, past Yanis, who stepped back and out of sight.

The consultant began examining her, and through the muffled sounds as she began to fade into unconsciousness, she heard him say something about her placenta, about blood loss, about losing them all.

She tried to fight. She tried to stay awake. She tried to hold on to whatever shred of control she had left. But it was to no avail. Her eyes closed, and all the pain, the fear, the blood and the panic began to drift away until it did not exist at all.

Yanis sat in the waiting room, his head in his hands, utter despair washing through his body. Was it true what she'd said? *Had* he made her do this? Had he forced her to do something she hadn't wanted?

He didn't think he had.

But what if he'd done it without realising? What if he'd made her feel she *had* to do this? What if his own desire to have healthy children after his losses had made him push her into a choice she wasn't ready for? Had he put her life at risk just so he could have children?

If he had, then he would never forgive himself if he lost her. The idea of losing her was… unbearable. Inconceivable. Heartbreaking.

And that other thing she'd said—that last thing about Giselle. Did Sam truly believe that of him? He felt sick at the thought. It had never been like that between him and Giselle. He had done what he could. What she had allowed him to do. She had been the one to push *him* away!

What was happening? Was he going to lose them all? Why wasn't anyone coming out to tell him what was going on?

Whenever he performed surgeries and knew there was family waiting outside, he would periodically send out a nurse to keep them updated. Why was no one updating him? He hoped it was because they were so busy saving Sam and the babies' lives that no one was free to take a quick stroll outside and let him know what was happening.

If that was the case, then so be it. He'd rather they were doing that. But… He sighed, letting out a long-drawn breath. It would be nice to know *something*.

He couldn't quite believe he was in this position. Sitting there. Waiting to hear whether Sam and the babies were okay. Whether they were even *alive*. Whether he would even have the chance to explain to her that she was so terribly wrong about him and Giselle.

After the ablation had gone so well, he'd imagined he'd finally get to be a father, sitting at Sam's bedside, holding her hand and mopping her brow as she laboured and gave birth. He'd dreamed of that moment. Fantasised about it—about how beautiful it would be to see his children come into the world.

But even that was being denied him now. All these physical things were going wrong...

Why was she trying to blame him?

Because she's scared, and scared people lash out.

He'd never even made it out of the starting gate as a father. Ever. There had always been a problem, always a fault, always something devastating waiting for him around the corner. They should never have gone ahead with this. The risk was too great. It wasn't worth it.

Was Sam right? Was there something so fundamentally broken in both of them that they couldn't have children without risking their lives? He'd already lost three babies. He'd already been through hell. He'd already been left alone and broken. Was he doomed to have the same thing happen? Could he go through that devastation again?

No. I have to believe that Mr Meyer is saving them all.

He had to believe it. But he didn't know how. Didn't know how to sit with the guilt and the fear and the worry.

Yanis's pager suddenly went off, and he grabbed a phone and dialled the number.

Jahira's parents were still waiting for an update on how the surgery had gone. He'd not had a chance to speak to them—he'd rushed straight here with Sam.

He went over to the receptionist and told her that he'd be in Neuro, talking to the young girl's parents—reassuring them—and that they should page him when they had news. He wouldn't be long.

Yanis couldn't help Sam right now, but he could help that girl's worried parents. They had to be going out of their minds, wanting to know if the surgery had been a success, and he had let them down. He had put his personal feelings for Sam and the babies over his patient's family.

There's a pattern showing here. I'm selfish. Selfish beyond belief. Maybe Sam is right in that.

No one could hate him more in that moment than he hated himself.

Jahira's parents stood as he approached them in the neuro ICU. Yanis shook their hands and introduced himself.

'How is she doing?' asked her father.

'She's doing very well. The surgery went as expected, though we were unable to replace the bone flap due to some swelling, which we hope will go down in the next day or so.'

'What happens then?'

'Then we take her back into Theatre and replace it. For now, as you can see, she is all bandaged up, and there's a marker there for all staff, to remind them to be careful.'

'When will she wake up?'

'It could be any time. Surgery on the brain affects people differently. Plus, she has the trauma of the accident to deal with, so it may be a little while longer.'

'She's a good girl. She always wears her helmet. I don't understand why she didn't have it on.'

Yanis nodded. 'People do things sometimes that don't make any sense.'

'Will she be okay when she wakes up?'

'We don't know for sure. She received quite a severe knock to her brain, and it was injured. We removed the clot and repaired what we could, but we'll only know when she wakes up.'

'And if there's a problem?'

'Then she'll need to go through some physio. Some rehabilitation work. We have a very good department here at Barney's.'

'She has her whole life ahead of her, you know...?'

He nodded. He did know. He felt that way about his babies. He'd already lost three. Extinguished before they could even begin. Life wasn't fair.

'Jahira was our miracle baby,' said her mother. 'A complete surprise. I'd been told I couldn't get pregnant and… Well, she's our whole world.'

'I understand. Do you have any other questions?'

'No, thank you. You're busy. I'm sure you have other patients to worry about.'

He nodded and walked away towards the reception area, where he sank down into a chair and held his head in his hands before checking his bleeper, to make sure that the battery hadn't gone flat and that he hadn't missed anything.

These twins were *his* miracle babies. A complete surprise. Unexpected. Was it possible that he'd got so close to the finishing line, but wouldn't make it across? Had he somehow failed Sam in his duty to look after her? *Was* this all his fault? If it was—if he lost any of them—he would never forgive himself.

At that moment his bleeper sounded and he almost jumped out of his skin. Checking the number, he saw it was Theatre. He had to take a moment to steady his hand and take some deep breaths to slow his heart rate, before he picked up the phone and dialled through.

'This is Yanis Baptiste.'

Sam woke reluctantly. She'd been having a lovely dream. Something about riverboats and lying back in the sunshine with her fingertips trailing in the water, creating ripples that made music. It had been relaxing. Peaceful... But as she came back to awareness and blinked open her eyes, she heard the beep of monitors, smelled the familiar aroma of hospital and suddenly remembered what had been happening before she was put to sleep.

Tilting her head, she looked down at her abdomen. The mountain she was used to seeing was gone. Her belly was substantially less domed than it had been the last time she'd seen it.

The realisation that her babies had been delivered hit hard. But they weren't in the room. There were no cots. Then she realised that someone was holding her hand and she saw Yanis, saw his tear-stained face, and her heart broke into a million pieces. She must have lost the babies.

'No!' She sobbed, hiccupping in great breaths.

'Sam… Sam, it's okay.'

'It's not okay! They're gone! They're gone and it's all my fault!'

'No, no, they're not gone. They're okay. They're in the NICU. They're alive!'

She stopped to stare at Yanis. Had he really said what she thought he'd said?

'What?'

'They're alive, Sam. They're doing great. We're parents.'

'We are?'

Yanis let go of her hand to reach inside his pocket for his mobile phone. He tapped at the screen to bring up his gallery. 'Look—I have pictures.'

She took his phone, noting a cannula in the back of her left hand that she hadn't noticed before, and gazed in sheer delight at the photos Yanis had taken of their two girls, lying side by side in incubators.

'How long have I been out?'

'All this happened yesterday. They had a little difficulty breathing when they came out, but Mr Meyer said it was just the shock of sudden delivery. They're going to be fine!'

'They are?' Sam burst into tears again. 'I want to see them.' She tried to sit up.

'You need to recover a bit more first. You lost a lot of blood. When your transfusion is done you can go up there.'

'What happened?'

'The placenta happened.'

'It came away?'

'*Oui.* I thought I was going to lose you all...'

'You could have.' She wiped her eyes. 'I shouldn't have blamed you. I was frightened. I thought I was going to lose the babies, and I thought that if that happened then I'd lose you, too.'

'You would never have lost me,' he said, with such certainty that she just had to stare at him for a minute.

'No? You lost Giselle. I thought...' She looked away, ashamed of her thoughts, ashamed of admitting her feelings. 'I thought that maybe you'd told me Giselle had walked away to save face—that *you* might have left *her*. To find someone who *could* give you a child.'

'You thought that of me?' He looked shocked. 'That I could be so cruel and selfish?'

She shook her head, wiping away more tears. 'I didn't believe it, Yanis! Honestly, I didn't. But it crossed my mind. Briefly. I'm not proud of it. And once I'd thought it, I couldn't get it out of my mind! I've always been used by other people. Used to get things that *they* want. When you told me about what had happened, all I could think was that you'd do anything to have a child. Anything to have a family. She couldn't give that to you.'

'So you thought I'd walked away from her?'

'Maybe… I don't know! I was scared. Afraid of being alone. I thought that if I prepared for it, if I justified it in my mind, then I wouldn't be so shocked if you *did* walk away. But it was because I didn't want to lose you. Because I thought that maybe you were with me just because of the babies.'

'*Sam!*' He shook his head. But then he

looked at her, imploring her with his eyes. 'I *love* you. I've loved you for a long time. If the worst had come to the worst and we'd lost our girls, you still would have had me. I promise you that.'

'You love me?' His words seemed impossible.

He nodded, smiling. 'I do. And there is nothing in the whole wide world that will change that. I've been so scared, Sam. Scared of losing you all. Not just the babies. The idea of losing you... I could never have coped with that.'

Sam smiled back, reaching out for his face, stroking it, feeling the fear and the shame drift away. 'Can you ever forgive me for thinking all that?' she asked.

'There's nothing to forgive. You were scared. People do and say strange things sometimes when they're scared.'

He thought of Jahira. The girl who'd always worn a helmet but hadn't yesterday. Had she been scared? Had she set out in a rush because something had scared her?

'The surgery I did. That last patient. Jahira. Was she okay?' asked Sam.

Yanis nodded. 'She's fine. I'm going to go in tomorrow and replace the skull flap. The swelling has come down.'

'That's good. That's very good.'

'This is what I love about you.'

She smiled. 'What?'

'How much you care for other people. Even when you're at risk yourself, you still worry about others.'

'I'm not at risk any more.'

'Thankfully.'

'I have you. I have my girls. It all ended okay.'

'It ended more than "okay". It ended perfectly.'

She reached out and took his hand. 'You've been so patient. So strong. You've been there for me despite all my fears, as well as carrying a burden of your own. I love you so much. *Je t'aime*, Yanis.'

He raised an eyebrow. 'You've learned French?'

'Un peu.'

Yanis laughed. 'We might have to work on your accent!'

* * *

Yanis wheeled her into the NICU, and even though her heart was already full of love, it overflowed at the sight of her two girls, lying next to each other in one incubator.

'We had them in their own incubators to start with, but they wouldn't settle. I think they missed each other, so we put them together,' said a nurse.

Her two girls were identical. The same dark hair, the same noses, same mouths. They were beautiful, lying facing one another.

'Would you like to hold them?' asked the nurse.

'Can we?' Sam asked.

The nurse nodded. 'Let me get you a pillow.'

She gave Sam a pillow and then opened up an incubator to get out the first baby, laying her in Sam's arms within her open top, so that they could be skin to skin.

'And one for Dad?'

Yanis nodded, smiling, ripping off his tie and opening up his shirt, too.

'I'll leave you to it. I'll be just over at the nurses' station if you need me.'

'Thank you.'

Sam and Yanis both sat holding a baby, their gazes taking in everything about their daughters.

'Look at how they hold their hands the same way,' said Sam.

Both babies held one arm across their stomach and the other up by their face.

'We need to choose their names,' she said.

'We do. What do you think of Charlotte?' Yanis suggested.

She nodded. 'I like that… Charlotte Emmeline?'

Yanis looked up at her and, remembering their patient in Paris, nodded. 'I like it.'

'And this little one… What about Aurelie? Or Camille?'

'Or both? Aurelie Camille… That's beautiful.'

'Charlotte and Aurelie Gordon-Baptiste.' She laughed. 'That's quite a mouthful.'

'It could just be Baptiste.'

Sam frowned. 'What do you mean?'

'You could marry me.'

Sam held her breath.

Had he really just suggested marriage?

Could she imagine herself married to Yanis?

Yes, she could!

She laughed. 'I could...'

'Is that a yes?'

She thought back to the beginning. To that night when they'd first got involved and how she'd told herself always to be sure of her decisions. This one was easy to make.

'It is. *Oui.*'

Yanis leaned forward and kissed her. Softly. Gently. His eyes were full of love.

'You can still keep your surname, though. You don't have to take mine.'

'Are you kidding me?' She leaned forward and stroked his face. 'I want the whole world to know that I'm yours.'

* * * * *

LET'S TALK
Romance

For exclusive extracts, competitions
and special offers, find us online:

f facebook.com/millsandboon

⬡ @millsandboonuk

🐦 @millsandboon

Or get in touch on 0844 844 1351*

For all the latest titles coming soon,
visit millsandboon.co.uk/nextmonth